BETWE
CLOSE

By the time he reached the landing his nerve-ends were screaming and Tony Clark, veteran of fifteen years in the force, was on edge. Too late he realised that his enthusiasm to find McLaughlin had overtaken his better judgement. Why hadn't he brought Harry with him? Why hadn't he waited for Mo to get back from Brighton? What on earth was the hurry? . . .

But had he not paused to consider the finer points of why he happened to be alone in an isolated farmhouse in the middle of nowhere, he might not, one minute later, have found himself lying flat on his stomach praying for his life.

'Lie down!' commanded the voice behind him. Tony turned round to find that the voice meant business. The man standing in the corner of the room was holding a shotgun, and it was aimed, in an expert manner, at the back of his head.

Also from Warner Books

BETWEEN THE LINES:
Close protection

· TOM McGREGOR

WARNER BOOKS

A *Warner* Book

First published in Great Britain in 1994 by Warner Books

Copyright © Tom McGregor 1994

The moral right of the author has been asserted.

A CIP catalogue record for this book
is available from the British Library.

ISBN 0 7515 1266 4

Photoset in North Wales by
Derek Doyle & Associates, Mold, Clwyd.
Printed and bound in Great Britain by
Clays Ltd, St Ives plc

Warner Books
A Division of
Little, Brown and Company (UK)
Brettenham House
Lancaster Place
London WC2E 7EN

BETWEEN THE LINES: CLOSE PROTECTION

1

Bitter. Every time Tony Clark thought about it, that's how he felt. He knew he should try to forget about it; he knew bitterness served no purpose other than to destroy from within, but each time he cast his mind back to the events of six months ago, he was gripped anew by the seething, impotent emotion that he found impossible to quell. The emotion that left him with an anger as fierce as it had been on the day when he knew his career in the force was over. Except they no longer called it a force. Now it was the 'police service'. Less unpleasant sounding, they claimed. Tony gripped the steering-wheel of his elderly Saab and grinned without humour. He knew all about unpleasantness.

'The Attorney-General,' his Guv'nor had said, 'has decided that the criminal charges against you may be difficult to prove and that they're unlikely to secure a conviction.' Tony had been unable to disguise his delight at those words – not least because he had known how much they must have cost David Graves to utter. He had smiled – smirked – at his hated boss but Graves had

1

remained impassive. Then he had wiped the smile off Tony's face with his next words. 'But,' he continued, 'they feel it's worth having a go.'

Tony felt as if he had been hit. The words hurt more than the accusation of first-degree murder that had led to his suspension in the first place. He looked at Graves aghast. Graves smirked back. 'However,' he added, 'if you were to resign . . .'

'*Resign?*'

'. . . then they would drop the criminal charges and we would drop the disciplinary charges.'

'If you want me out, you're going to have to drive me out. I'm not just giving up something that has been my life.' Tony had not been exaggerating. 'The job', and latterly CIB, had indeed been his life.

Graves didn't even have the grace to wipe the supercilious expression off his face. 'It's your choice, Anthony,' he had said as he walked away. 'But personally, I think you've got a bargain.'

There had, of course, been neither bargain nor choice. Tony had been around long enough to know that he had to resign – and therein lay the injustice that still left him bitter. Cursing at the London traffic as he crawled in the direction of Maureen Connell's house, he reflected on the long, messy process that had led to his 'resignation'. His work as a detective superintendent at the CIB – the Complaints Investigations Bureau that dealt with corruption within the force itself – had left him under no illusions about power and its misuse. Policemen abusing their positions of trust were nothing new. Nor were coppers who turned a blind eye to misdemeanours in return

2

for a backhander. But policemen who got themselves unwittingly mixed up in 'big boys' games' involving manipulation by the Special Branch and MI5 and, indirectly, the IRA, were a different matter. They had to play by unwritten big boys' rules and Tony hadn't been armed with those rules when he had rushed in good faith into a situation from which he had been lucky to escape alive. Instead, he had emerged with one leg shattered by a high-velocity bullet, several broken fingers, a bloody face, a dead body beside him and – ultimately – no job. Resign, or face serious criminal charges. Someone was going to have to play the scapegoat and as it would have to be either Tony or someone from MI5, there was no contest.

He still smarted when he thought of the expression on Gravesie's face. At least he could think of him as Gravesie again. Latterly, he had been obliged to call him Guv'nor – and that had really hurt. The day his equal David Graves became his boss had been the day his career in CIB had started to look shaky. They hated each other. Sooner or later, there was bound to be a parting of the ways. And it had happened sooner than either of them had anticipated. Graves was still chief superintendent of the CIB – and Clark was now a freelance security consultant.

Tony Clark Associates had, he thought, a nice ring to it – even if the word 'associates' was stretching the truth. His only associate was Harry Naylor, his one-time right-hand man at CIB. Harry's career had, of late, spiralled downhill with a speed equalled only by the rapid deterioration of his private life. It would have surprised many who knew Tony that he cared deeply for Harry, and that he also felt responsible for him and many of his woes. Tony, while often seen as a maverick, as a vain and selfish man who thought only of himself and his career, possessed – in spades – an unswerving loyalty to his friends. And Harry was, above all else, a friend.

As the traffic thinned out at Shepherd's Bush, Tony accelerated and collected his thoughts about the matter in hand; about the reason why he was heading towards Maureen Connell's house. Mo, the third member of his team at CIB, had suffered a fate not dissimilar to that of Tony and Harry. Prior to Tony's 'resignation', she had been promoted to inspector and transferred to another unit. Yet Maureen's new career had been short-lived. Tony liked to think that an unseen guiding hand, the pupper-master of inevitability, was trying to tell the three of them that they should not be separated. That way he could salve his conscience. But, deep down, he knew better. He had been directly responsible for Maureen losing her job, and he felt deeply, horribly guilty about it. Hence the unannounced visit. And hence the chilled bottle of Veuve Cliquot lying in the passenger seat. It wasn't much, he knew, in the way of compensation, but it was a gesture. It was also a preliminary to opening new and delicate negotiations about Maureen's future; about justifying the 's' in Tony Clark Associates. Tony desperately wanted Maureen on board. Maureen, he suspected, would be wary.

He grinned ruefully to himself as he turned into her street. Wary, he thought, was putting it mildly.

Maureen would probably be apoplectic with rage at the idea of joining his business.

She was, in fact, neither wary nor apoplectic: she was absent. It was Kate Roberts who answered the door and who was the unimpressed recipient of Tony's most endearing and, he hoped, irresistible smile.

'Kate!' Tony's disappointment was brief and easily disguised. He liked Kate almost as much as he liked Maureen. The fact that the two women were lovers no longer surprised him. People's private lives, he had long ago decided, were their own and nobody else's business, and if Maureen wanted to live with another woman then that was all right by him. It was, in fact, more than all right. For two years he had been making advances to Maureen and had been privately puzzled and not a little annoyed by her resistance. Only when she had declared her sexuality to him did he understand. And then he had silently cursed himself for not twigging before. Tony, open-minded in almost everything else, still believed that if a woman didn't find him irresistible, she had to be a lesbian.

Kate returned Tony's smile. Yet her own smile didn't reach her eyes. 'Hello, Tony.'

He expected her to say something else. She didn't. 'Is . . . is Mo about?'

'No.'

'Oh.' Tony suddenly felt like a teenager let down on his first date. He grinned feebly at Kate's inscrutable expression. 'Ah. Job-hunting, is she?'

'No. She's got a job.'

'*What*? A job? Already?' This was most definitely not what Tony had expected. Maureen had been dismissed a mere two weeks before. He felt, unaccountably, rather peeved. Kate couldn't help grinning at his stricken expression. 'Yes. She's been taken on by a TV company.'

'Oh? What's she doing?'

'Some sort of investigation. I'm afraid I don't know much about it.' Relenting in the face of his crestfallen look, she gestured behind her. 'Look, you're welcome to come in but I'm meeting a client for lunch and—'

'No, no. It's all right. Really.' He grinned and raised a hand in awkward farewell. 'It'll wait.' As he turned back towards his car he remembered the bottle of champagne in his other hand. He turned on his heel and caught Kate before she closed the door behind him. 'Look,' he raised the bottle, 'please give her this, will you? It was just a sort of gesture, y'know, to celebrate her – um – new opportunities.'

'Thanks, Tony. Sweet of you. I know she'll appreciate it.'

Kate cast a lingering, thoughtful look at Tony's retreating back before closing the door softly but firmly behind her. Then she eyed the bottle with something approaching distaste. Tony's unannounced arrival, his awkward 'gesture', made her feel uneasy. She knew that Tony was fond of Maureen; she also knew that he felt, in his own repressed way, responsible for her ignominious and painful departure from the force. Yet somewhere in the back of her mind, he had set alarm bells ringing. Tony, then Harry, and now Maureen. Three ex-colleagues down on their luck.

She knew that as a team they had worked with an almost intuitive understanding when they were all with CIB. She knew that they had enjoyed working with each other. And she strongly suspected that Tony's visit was prompted by ulterior motives.

Kate Roberts had found it difficult to adjust to being the partner of a policewoman. When she had first met Maureen, she hadn't realised that doing the job actually meant living the job. When Mo had been with CIB, she had never really, in spirit, been off duty: there had always been a private part of her mind that remained on the alert, that kept her attuned to a job that was not only demanding but also made her relatively unpopular within the force. True, the job had carried a certain amount of kudos, but it also meant that others in the force were mindful that, should an investigation go wrong, should one of them be suspected of some nefarious activity, then it would have been Maureen and her team who would be investigating them.

Kate had been immensely relieved when Maureen had been promoted to inspector and transferred. Tony Clark had already been removed; Harry was unhappy both at home and at work, and Kate felt that a change of scene and more responsibility would be the best thing for Mo. What she hadn't counted on was Mo's unswerving belief in and unshakable loyalty towards her ex-colleagues. What she hadn't reckoned on was Harry's resignation and subsequent teaming-up with Tony – and the request, from the newly formed Tony Clark Associates, that Maureen access the Police National Computer without authorisation. Kate knew enough about Mo's job by then to realise that such an action could have dire results. She had told Mo she was a fool: Mo had replied that they were all working on the same side, that she had accessed the computer to help a murder investigation and to protect a police witness. That much had, in fact, been true. But nothing she could say could hide the fact that she had logged into classified information. And no amount of denials could convince her superiors that she had not passed that information on to Tony Clark. What Maureen, like Tony before her, had failed to realise was that the higher up you were in the force, the more there was to cover up; that at certain levels you came under the aegis of Special Branch and MI5, both of whom had rules of their own. And, unwittingly, both she and Tony Clark Associates had stumbled into an area where those rules applied.

Kate walked into the kitchen, opened the fridge, and deposited the bottle of champagne on the top shelf. Again she looked at it as if it were the harbinger of new and unwelcome news. Then she shook her head and grinned to herself. She was, she knew, being fanciful. The champagne was a peace offering, and a final reminder that Mo's days of being exhausted and upset by the demands of a police career were at last over. Perhaps, she thought, Mo's contract with the TV company would lead to something more permanent – and less stressful.

So many possibilities, mused Kate as she prepared to leave the house for her meeting. The only certainty was that the words Special Branch and

MI5 would never again serve to disrupt her life and endanger Mo's. She quelled any unease about Tony's visit with the thought that those days were now firmly in the past. They could, she thought, celebrate their passing by cracking open the champagne tonight.

Thirty seconds after she let herself out of the house, the bottle of champagne, warmed by the sun through Tony's windscreen, shaken up by both his and Kate's hands and then plunged into a too-cold fridge, enjoyed a celebration all of its own. With an ominous and very loud bang, it exploded.

2

Maureen sat forward in her seat, her face a study in concentration as she watched the video monitor in front of her. The quality of the footage was poor, suggesting that the camcorder had been held by an amateur, yet it was the content, not the quality, that commanded her attention. Her trained eye took in the whole image as it swerved uncertainly to cover the broad sweep of a seafront, easily identifiable as Brighton. Then, abruptly, the picture changed to show a young mother and a little girl smiling self-consciously. That particular picture said it all: here was a holiday film, taken by a proud father, recording every moment of a child's first seaside outing. Maureen edged closer to the screen as the child opened her mouth to say something. Yet the words were drowned by a car horn in the distance and by the screech of brakes. On the film, both mother and child turned in the direction of the disruption. So, evidently, did the father: for a few seconds the film was entirely blurred and its images unidentifiable. Watching it would have been comical were it not for the fact that the film was still picking up sound – the sound of indistinct

10

shouts followed by very loud, very distinct gunfire. A shiver ran down Maureen's back. It was a sound she was all too familiar with.

Then the film became a series of kaleidoscopic, blurred images suggesting that the cameraman was running. A few seconds later the picture suddenly leaped into focus as the camera zoomed in in time to catch four men, all dressed in black and all masked, standing over three prone bodies lying on the pavement outside the Grand Hotel. They surveyed the bodies briefly and professionally and then ran, obviously unaware of the camera, towards two nearby cars. Even before they had closed all the doors, the vehicles accelerated and sped off into the distance. As they disappeared, the camera returned to the pavement, near the scene of the shootings and revealed a man getting slowly and uneasily to his feet. Then he bent to pick something up. As he did so, Maureen sucked in her breath. He was bending down to retrieve his hat – or rather, his helmet. As the camera focused more clearly on the man, Maureen clocked his uniform and identified him as a police constable. He ran over to the still-inert bodies as a clutch of police and security men came rushing out of the main entrance of the hotel. Then the image faded and the screen went blank.

Maureen exhaled deeply, sat back in her chair, and turned to the woman sitting beside her. 'Where on earth,' she began, 'did you get that from? I've never seen that clip before.'

Sarah Teale's expression matched the seriousness of the film they had just viewed, yet her eyes could not hide a sparkle of triumph. 'I don't think

11

anybody's seen it before. It arrived here in a plain brown envelope. No message. Nothing. Just,' she pointed at the monitor, 'that tape.'

'Hmm.' Maureen was silent for a moment. 'And apart from the man who filmed it, the policeman was the only witness to the shootings?'

'No.' Sarah leaned forward and addressed the third person in the room. 'Could you run my interview, please?'

The editor, none too pleased that the two women had taken over his editing suite, busied himself with the machinery in front of him. Then a picture, much clearer and more professional than anything that had gone before, appeared on the monitor. It appeared to have been filmed in a hotel bedroom, and showed a distressed-looking chambermaid talking directly to camera. Twisting her hands in front of her, she spoke with passion in answer to a question from the unseen interviewer. 'They didn't,' she said, 'have time to do *anything*. I saw them there, frozen, with their hands in the air and . . . and I think I heard one of them shouting something like, "Don't shoot, boys!" '

Her interviewer, revealed by her voice as Sarah herself, repeated the words. 'Don't shoot, boys?'

'Yes,' said the chambermaid. 'And then – and then they just started shooting. They never stood a chance,' she added with vehemence. 'Then after the shooting, the soldiers went up to them and – well, they *kicked* the bodies. And then I saw them shoot one of them again, three times, in the head.' Her voice high with disbelief, the chambermaid looked straight into the camera and then that image, too, faded and the screen went blank.

There was a brief silence in the editing suite and then Sarah spoke. 'We'll voice-over the chambermaid's words with the images from the home video. So we'll hear the witness while viewing what she saw.'

'Powerful,' said Maureen.

'But not powerful enough. We need the other witness. The policeman. Constable Clive Barrett. Nobody could deny he was there.'

'And that's where I come in?'

'That is indeed where you come in.' Sarah rose to her feet and smiled at the editor, who was casting ever more irritated looks in their direction. 'Thanks, Jim, for showing that again.'

'No problem,' he lied.

'Shall we go to my office,' asked Sarah as Maureen stood up, 'and I'll fill you in on the background?'

Maureen smiled a thin smile. She knew, of course, most of the background to the story. Most people did, and every ex-police officer did. The shooting incident had taken place in Brighton in 1992. The newspapers had had a field day with what they saw as an attempted rerun of the Brighton bombings of 1984, and the tabloids had run gleeful headlines about the three IRA men being gunned down by the SAS. It had been hailed as a triumph and a justification of the so-called 'shoot-to-kill' tactics of Britain's specialist forces which had recently been a political hot potato. Had the SAS not acted promptly, the implication was, the Grand Hotel and the Conservative Party Conference would again have been devastated by terrorist activity. Mo rather resented the implication

13

that she would know less about it than this cool blonde who was, Mo suspected, barely into her thirties.

Once in her office, Sarah smiled at Mo and offered her a cup of coffee. 'I won't insult you,' she said, 'by going over the Brighton affair itself. You were, I take it, in the force at the time?' Maureen nodded in affirmation as Sarah smiled and continued, 'What you'll want to know is the background of the series we're making. It's a six-parter on shoot-to-kill, all round the world. Covert operations, disappearances – wherever the state sidesteps the rules. Episode four is the one which deals with Brighton.'

Maureen, slightly alarmed by Sarah's matter-of-fact tones in talking about such a controversial issue, did her best to hide her surprise. 'Bit contentious, isn't it?' she offered. 'I mean, how do you decide where law enforcement ends and shoot-to-kill begins?'

But Sarah had obviously done her homework. 'The SAS rules of engagement for the military commander in Brighton were quite plain. They were there to assist the police in arresting the terrorists. They were not to use more force than was necessary, and were to give a clear warning before opening fire.' She paused and looked at Maureen. 'The terrorists were unarmed.'

'Yes.' Maureen had forgotten that. 'I remember.'

'And you'll remember that the Government was not at its most popular at that time. The party was screaming for blood, for something to boost its public image. The shootings,' she emphasised, 'could not have come at a better time. The Government gained six percentage points in the polls overnight. They got standing ovations all round.' Sarah smiled a grim little smile and pushed a pile of newspaper cuttings towards Maureen. 'There were enough jingoistic headlines to sink the Belgrano all over again.'

Maureen glanced at the headlines. They were all from the tabloids and screamed out a variety of confidently unsubtle messages. 'TORIES CHEER NEW GET-TOUGH POLICY,' ran one. 'BRIGHTON REPLAY 3-0,' said a particularly direct banner above a fairly graphic photograph of the bodies. 'DEAD!' boasted another, 'BRAVE SQUADDIES AMBUSH IRA KILLERS.' 'SAS FOIL IRA OUTRAGE,' ran the only headline with any particular interest in the truth. She grimaced and pushed the cuttings back towards Sarah. 'It was the best news the Home Secretary had all year, if I remember. He really pushed home the message that they'd stopped the IRA carrying out a rerun of 1984.'

'That,' replied Sarah pointedly, 'is the official line. What really interests me, however, is the fact that PC Barrett was not called at the inquest. The hotel's security cameras had been switched off three minutes before the shootings, so there was no official record of Barrett having been there.'

'Until that video surfaced?'

'Precisely.'

'Odd that it should arrive anonymously at this office just as you're starting the shoot-to-kill series.' Maureen's Scottish accent helped to emphasise the dry sarcasm of her words.

Sarah grinned at Maureen's expression. 'Oddly

enough, we've had a lot of co-operation on this one.' She paused. 'From Special Branch.'

Maureen had been around long enough not to be surprised about who Special Branch did, and did not, co-operate with. They operated by rules of their own. Big boys' rules, Tony had once called them. 'And who was it,' she replied, 'who recommended me?'

'I'm a journalist, Maureen. Don't ask me to divulge my sources.' Then Sarah looked at her watch. 'In fact,' she declared artlessly, 'I'm off to interview a Special Branch officer in a few minutes. Naturally, he can't be identified.'

Maureen nodded non-committally. 'Look dear,' she felt like saying, 'don't try to impress me. I'm unimpressionable.' That, in fact, was untrue. She had been highly impressed by Sarah Teale until the girl had started to boast about her contacts. Friendly, direct and obviously highly efficient, she was the sort of person with whom Maureen enjoyed working. Mo smiled at Sarah and decided to overlook her last remark. 'Why,' she asked, 'are Special Branch so keen to help a documentary on shoot-to-kill?'

Sarah shrugged. 'Sour grapes? If you remember, MI5 took over anti-terrorist work from Special Branch soon after the Brighton incident. It was going that way before, but Brighton clinched it for MI5.' Maureen nodded. She did remember.

'So,' continued Sarah, 'Branch rather conveniently led me to PC Barrett. The only problem is, he's not keen to appear in the programme.' She smiled at Maureen. 'I was hoping that, with your experience in getting coppers to confess, you might stand a better chance of persuading him.'

'Hmm. He's obviously not keen to be identified if he saw the shootings and kept quiet about it for two years.' She looked challengingly at Sarah. 'He's obviously been sat on.'

'That's what I thought too.'

'But now Special Branch have led you straight to him?'

Sarah looked at her watch again and stood up. 'Something like that,' she said vaguely. 'As far as I'm concerned, Brighton was a clear case of shoot first and don't ask questions later.' She turned to Maureen, now also standing. 'But it'll sound better coming from PC Barrett's lips. Apart from the SAS, he's the only person who'd know if proper warnings were given.' Sarah gestured towards the door. 'If you come with me, I'll introduce you to my production manager. She'll give you the details of where to find him.'

Maureen had plenty of time for reflection as she drove down to Brighton to talk to PC Clive Barrett. And, she reflected, not on the case in hand, but on the recent past.

The last two weeks had been a nightmare. Like Tony Clark, she felt bitter at the treatment she had received from the Met, but there was still a raw edge to her bitterness. She still felt vulnerable, almost naked; deprived of the armour with which she had unknowingly surrounded herself for most of her working life. She had rarely paused to consider that, as a policewoman, she was part of a special group, that she was someone who stood out to the public, but who was – for all the dangers inherent in her job – protected by the security blanket of safety in numbers. Or, she thought wryly, of honour amongst thieves. Every group was, in some way, a law unto itself, and the force was no exception. And Maureen had been found guilty of breaking that law. That she had broken it because she was committed to pursuing the course of justice had cut no ice with her superiors. They were – as she had told them in no uncertain terms – concerned with image rather than law and order. And then they had ripped away her security blanket and Maureen was left with no job, no redundancy, no self-esteem and, of course, no security.

Kate had been a tower of strength and had encouraged Mo to take things easy, not to rush into anything and to spend time thinking seriously about which direction she wished to move in career-wise. Maureen, initially too shell-shocked to argue, had quietly acquiesced. Neither of them had voiced what was uppermost in both their minds: the fact that Maureen's dismissal from the Met left her in the same position as Tony and Harry Naylor. Maureen knew that Kate would hate her to join the grandiosely named and severely under-employed firm of Tony Clark Associates. Apart from the fact that Kate blamed Tony for Mo's present situation and that Tony's 'firm' seemed willing to take on any form of demeaning work, including hotel security, Kate was jealous of the intimate though non-sexual relationship Maureen had with both men. They had a bond of shared experience which created a barrier Kate could never penetrate. And now that all three of them had been forced into rethinking their careers, the bond was stronger.

But Tony had not pressured Mo into anything. He too had been a pillar or support and a shoulder to cry on, and so had Harry. No mention was made of Mo joining them, and she had silently thanked them for that.

The phone call from Encounter Productions had come completely out of the blue. Kate had suspected Tony's involvement, but her fears had been unfounded. A discreet phone call to Harry had established that Tony Clark Associates had never heard of Encounter. Harry had, in fact, been rather miffed that Kate was finding herself free-lance work so soon. He had left a question-mark in the air on the matter of helping Kate with her inquiries. She had left it in the air, and had also cautioned Harry not to tell Tony about the job. Harry wasn't as volatile as Tony: where he had been miffed, Tony would be livid, jealous and racked with doubts about his own capabilities and reputation. He would, of course, on the surface, pretend to be only mildly interested. Maureen smiled quietly to herself as she sped towards Brighton. Tony liked to think of himself as enigmatic. As far as Mo was concerned, he was transparent.

She didn't need to exercise any great powers of detection to find PC Barrett. Brighton Central Police Station was not difficult to find. After reversing into a parking space opposite the station, Maureen lit a cigarette and examined the photograph of Barrett with which Mica Harris, Sarah's assistant, had provided her. He looked, she thought, like your archetypal copper. The only remarkable thing about him, she mused, was his presence at the shootings two years ago – and his subsequent silence about them.

An hour later, she found herself cursing Barrett's ordinariness: she almost failed to identify him as he sauntered out of the station. Leaping out of her car, she hurried after him as he ambled along the street.

'PC Barrett?'

Barrett, suddenly on the alert, turned round sharply. Maureen would not have been too flattered to know that he turned to face what he saw as an unremarkable, ordinary-looking redhead in, he guessed, her mid-thirties. He stared at her for a moment and then, with a gruff, 'That's right,' acknowledged her question.

'Maureen Connell.' Mo smiled and extended a hand. Without enthusiasm, Barrett shook it. 'I'm working on a TV documentary – with Sarah Teale – about the shootings here two years ago and—'

Barrett stopped her in mid-flow. 'I thought I'd made it clear to Miss Teale that I'm not getting involved.' He glared mutinously at her.

'I'm not a journalist,' she said brightly. 'I used to be with the Met. Detective inspector.'

Doubt now replaced suspicion in Barrett's expression. 'So how come you're working for TV?'

Maureen grinned. 'Well,' she said teasingly, 'I won't be for very much longer unless you can help me out. Can't I just beg ten minutes over a cup of coffee?'

'Well . . . seeing as you were once one of us . . .'

Ten minutes later Maureen looked at him

over a cloud of smoke. They were sitting in a dismal café on the seafront, drinking insipid coffee accompanied by rather stronger cigarettes. Maureen mulled over the comment Barrett had just made about the days prior to the shootings. 'So why,' she asked at length, 'was everyone so edgy? Why that year, rather than any other?'

Barrett shrugged. 'Word had got around that there were Micks in Brighton.' He grinned. 'It was the tarts, revving up for the Party Conference. They get a lot of trade then – and they're always good for gossip.'

Maureen was surprised. 'You had information there were terrorist suspects in Brighton – from prostitutes?'

Barrett looked evenly at her and took a slow drag on his cigarette. 'I didn't say terrorists. I said Micks. We were all on the alert.'

'Hmm. Did you see the incident clearly?'

'Very clearly. I saw four masked men jump out of cars and shoot the living shite out of three Paddies.'

'Jesus!'

'They could've been gangsters, armed robbers, whatever.' Barrett's voice lowered and his eyes took on a faraway look as he recalled the horror of that day. 'I didn't know who they were. All I thought was this is it – this is burial with full police honours.' He stubbed out his cigarette with unnecessary force. 'End of the line.'

Maureen grimaced in sympathy. 'I've had those moments myself,' she said. 'You're in shock for days, I know. You see the world differently after that.'

Her approach was paying off. Barrett was warming to her, glad of a sympathetic ear; glad to have someone who knew what it was all about. He leaned forward almost conspiratorially. 'You know, I actually spoke to two of them. The Provos, I mean. They pulled up in their car in front of the hotel and I told them to buzz off. No parking there, I said.'

'So they came back on foot, did they?'

'Yeah. And after I'd radioed in to report them. Irish accents, y'see, and we were all on edge.' Again his eyes took on a distant look. 'Five minutes later, they're walking down the seafront, so I go up to them, and next thing I know, it's Bosnia. Bullets flying.'

Maureen paused for a moment before asking, 'Did you hear any warnings before the SAS opened fire?'

Barrett looked strangely at her. 'Maybe I did. Maybe I didn't.'

'But they must have asked you at the inquest if you heard warnings?'

'I wasn't at the inquest.'

Maureen convincingly feigned complete surprise. 'You weren't?'

Barrett shrugged. 'Wouldn't have made a blind bit of difference if I was.'

Maureen leaned forward. 'What makes you say that?'

Barrett looked at her as if she were an idiot. 'Come on, Maureen. There was an active-service IRA unit on the streets of Brighton, planning to blow up the Tories. There's no way I was going to stand in that witness box and say I heard no warnings.'

'Hmm. I take your point. But did you *ask* to be allowed to avoid giving evidence?'

'Didn't have to. It was all looked after.'

'How do you mean?' Maureen suspected she knew exactly how, but she wanted to hear it in his own words.

'Special Branch told me to keep my head down, otherwise my fellow officers might forget to help me out when I'm in the shit.' Barrett looked at her as one police officer to another. 'I didn't need to be told. I wasn't going to rock the boat.'

Maureen nodded. She knew exactly the sort of pressure he was up against – and the probable repercussions if he refused to kow-tow to a higher authority. Tony had tried to go against the wishes of MI5, and look where that had got him. And Mo herself had also tried to buck the system in the name of justice with exactly the same results. No, she thought. She didn't blame Barrett one little bit. In retrospect she might have done likewise. Keeping stumm was, for the sake of one's career on the force, a much better option than rocking the boat.

She nodded reassuringly. 'That's fine.' She smiled encouragingly across the table. 'But Clive, what you've just told me – that's all we want to hear for the documentary.'

Barrett shook his head. 'Sorry Maureen. I plan to do another twenty years in "the job". I'm not going on TV to break the earth-shattering news that the SAS were trigger-happy.' Maureen had expected that. After a moment's thought, she remembered what he had said about the word on the street – from the girls on the street. 'What about the prostitutes?' she asked. 'Would it be worth me talking to them?'

Barrett looked at Maureen for a few silent seconds and then reached across for her cigarette packet. He grinned at her and then took out a pen. 'You can try,' he said as he wrote a name on the inside of the packet. Then he pushed it back towards her. 'But you didn't get this name from me.'

Maureen smiled in appreciation and looked at the name. 'Pamela Hewitt? Where will I find her?'

Barrett stood up to leave. 'In Brighton,' was all he said.

Maureen stayed in the café after Barrett had gone. She lit another cigarette and gazed pensively at the name he had given her. It was more than she had expected from him. After two years of total silence it was odd, she thought, that he should now divulge information that could potentially expose the Brighton affair as a whitewash, or worse, as an exercise in Government propaganda. But then again, perhaps it wasn't odd. Mo was ex-police – and the police force was not the same thing as Special Branch. If Barrett was harbouring any resentment towards the latter, a casual and anonymous tip-off to Maureen would serve to set the ball rolling in a game where Special Branch could well end up with more than a little egg on their faces.

Yet there was something about the whole enterprise that made her feel uneasy. How, she wondered, had Sarah Teale found out about her? Who had informed her of the recent availability of Maureen Connell, ex-detective inspector and late of the CIB – the perfect person to seek confidences from policemen? It hadn't been Tony or Harry. It was hardly likely to have been her ex-Guv'nor. She knew of only one other person who fitted the bill, and the thought of him sent a chill running through her. It couldn't, she told herself, be him. He only used people as pawns in dangerous games. But he did have contact with Special Branch, and, as Sarah Teale had said, Branch had been extremely helpful . . .

Dismissing the unpleasant thought from her mind, Maureen got up, went to the phone in the corner of the café and dialled the number of Encounter Productions. 'Sarah?' she asked after a long wait.

'Maureen!' Sarah sounded delighted to hear from her, and also slightly hassled. 'Progress?' she asked succinctly. 'Of a sort. Barrett's not going to talk. He's got too much to lose if he does.'

'Hmm,' Sarah sighed down the phone. 'Well, that leaves a nice big hole in my programme.' She paused for a moment. 'Look, Maureen, can I call you back? I'm in the middle of filming . . .'

'It's all right, this won't take long,' replied Maureen. 'I just want to know if you want me to follow up the lead he gave me.'

'He gave you a lead?'

'Yup. A local prostitute who had tipped him off about Irishmen in town. I don't know where it might get us but . . .'

'Follow it up, Maureen. Can you find her quickly?'

'Well . . .' Maureen hesitated before coming to the real point of her phone call. 'I suppose so. But I'll need to bring in someone to help me.'

Sarah didn't pause for even a second before assenting. 'Fine. Do what you need to – and keep me posted.'

'Great. Thanks, Sarah. Will do.' Maureen hung up and breathed a sigh of relief.

Then she fished in her purse for another coin. She was about to make Harry Naylor a happy man – and Tony Clark a very upset one.

In London, Sarah Teale also hung up, and then walked hurriedly back into the studio. She smiled apologetically at the cameraman and technicians, and at the man who she was interviewing. If he smiled back Sarah didn't notice. While her side of the table was well lit, the other side was in near-darkness and the man opposite her was revealed to the camera only in silhouette. Anonymity had been a strict condition of the interview. The man was a Special Branch officer.

'I'm sorry for the interruption,' she said crisply. Sitting down and turning to the cameraman, she nodded for the interview to continue. 'You were saying,' she said to the man in silhouette, 'that MI5 told the SAS that the terrorists were armed?'

'Yes.'

'And that there was an explosive device in the vicinity?'

'Yes.'

Sarah paused. 'And that information was wrong?'

'Not exactly,' replied the interviewee. 'The van

nearby was loaded with Semtex.'

'But there were no detonators?'

'No.'

Sarah had conducted enough interviews, had made enough documentaries to know that this one had all the elements of real drama. She tensed slightly before continuing. 'It does appear,' she said evenly, 'that while Special Branch was responsible for the safety of Government ministers at the conference, you were by-passed by Cabinet Office and MI5 when it came to the terrorists.'

'It was MI5's show.'

'But at that time,' persisted Sarah, 'it was Special Branch's job to provide and assess intelligence about IRA terrorists in Great Britain. Why, on this occasion, were you left out of the equation?'

'Under the '89 Act, MI5 comes directly under the authority of the Home Secretary. In the case of the Brighton shootings, there was a direct line between Cabinet Office and the MI5 officers on the ground.'

Again Sarah paused. 'And those officers,' she said with emphasis, 'are not accountable?'

'That is correct.'

Which brings us, thought Sarah, to the crux of the matter. She took a deep breath. 'If MI5 gave inadequate or misleading information to the SAS, might they also have misinformed Cabinet Office?'

'You'd have to ask them that.'

But Sarah was not to be deflected. 'Do you think, then, that Cabinet Office chose MI5 and the SAS to neutralise a perceived threat *because* they're unaccountable? Do you think they were chosen because Cabinet Office didn't want any questions asked – ever?'

'Yes.'

3

'The Guv,' said Harry as he met Maureen outside Brighton Station, 'was not a happy man.'

Maureen glared at him. 'Harry,' she said drily, 'for one thing he's not our Guv any more, and secondly, it's not my place to worry about whether or not he's happy.'

Harry turned round in surprise. 'Christ, Mo! Keep your hair on! He was only wondering why you were enlisting me rather than him for this job.'

Maureen stopped as they reached her car and looked her friend and ex-colleague in the eye. 'I want you, Harry, because it's more your line than Tony's. And I also want to get something clear. I've got a job, there's a problem, and I need your help. But that doesn't,' she added emphatically, 'mean it's the old firm back in business because it's not. I know Tony wants things that way and I know you're happy to freelance for him but I'm not going to do that. This is my case and I'd value your expertise. That's it.' She bent down to unlock the driver's door. 'And I don't want any old boys' talk about "the job". I'm out of the police, that's it. It's over. OK?'

If Harry had been surprised by Maureen's first remark about Tony, he was completely taken aback by her second outburst. Luckily, as Maureen slipped into the car and leaned over to unlock Harry's door, she missed the expression on his face: an expression of both astonishment and sadness. Then, as he too got into the car, he grinned suddenly. He knew why Maureen had reacted so violently to any mention of the old days. She was, he clicked, protesting too much. She was fighting against her own desire to see the old team back in business. Maureen noticed the grin. 'What's so funny?' she snapped. Harry shrugged and fished for a cigarette. 'Swings and roundabouts, I s'pose. The fact that I'm now working for you.'

'I don't find that a cause for amusement.'

'No, I don't suppose you would. Not when you're paying me a hundred a day plus expenses.'

This time it was she who couldn't suppress a smile. 'Is that so?'

'It is.'

'In which case, I expect you'd like me to tell you what you're being paid for.'

As they drove through town towards the seafront, Maureen briefed him on her meeting with Sarah Teale and subsequent encounter with PC Clive Barrett. 'What I really don't understand,' she finished, 'is why Special Branch told Barrett to keep quiet about the shootings and then, two years later, sent a TV company after him.'

'You're sure it's Special Branch who tipped off this Teale woman?'

'Yup. She was rather smug about it.'

'Stupid woman.'

Maureen cast him a sharp, sideways glance. 'No. No, she's not stupid. She's actually very smart. Although,' she conceded, 'being smug about your Special Branch contacts isn't very clever.'

'Mmm. D'you think,' asked Harry after a moment, 'that she knows where this could lead?'

'I *think* so, yes. But I'm not sure if she realises just how dirty people are prepared to play if their little games get discovered.'

'And who are the "people" in this case?'

'Well,' said Maureen. 'The Brighton shootings were a huge popularity boost for the Government, weren't they?'

The case, as Maureen had intimated and as Harry suspected, could lead them up some very interesting and potentially dangerous avenues, but two hours after Harry's arrival in Brighton, it had led him no further than a dismally depressing pub. The prostitute Pamela Hewitt was the only lead they had and the Sailor's Arms was, so Maureen had discovered, the sort of pick-up joint where people like Pamela plied their trade. Harry had been around long enough to suspect – and not to be insulted by the suspicion – that Maureen had chosen him to help because he blended into the general ambience of places like the Sailor's Arms. He had a lived-in face and a habitual, world-weary, 'seen-it-all' expression. On a good day he looked scruffy: on a bad one he could quite easily pass for seedy. Tony Clark, on the other hand, was younger, much better-looking, and would have looked hopelessly out of place in a pub like this. More to the point, he lacked the common touch.

Without meaning to, he always managed to antagonise the very people with whom he sought to establish a rapport. Had he, not Harry, walked into the Sailor's Arms, the overly made-up and over-the-hill barmaid would immediately have been suspicious.

She eyed Harry, on the other hand, without interest. 'Scotch, please, luv,' he said pleasantly.

'Ice?' She made it sound like a threat rather than an offer.

'No thanks.'

As she ambled over to the optic at the back of the bar, Harry glanced around the room. It was, he thought, a sad place. There were few customers, and none of them were couples. The single men stood at the other end of the bar, and three others occupied separate tables at the far end of the room. But it was the women who interested Harry. Or rather, the woman. She, like the barmaid, was painted, primped and primed for work – and it wasn't difficult to guess what line she was in. She smiled at Harry. He smiled back.

'Four pounds,' snarled the barmaid as she banged a thimbleful of amber liquid in front of him.

Harry turned round in horror. '*What*?'

'Four,' she repeated, '*pounds*.'

Harry handed her a fiver. 'And I'd like,' he said as she grabbed it, 'a receipt.'

As he sipped his drink he sensed that the woman at the table behind was approaching the bar. Sure enough, a slight movement to his right and the tap of a glass on the counter indicated her presence beside him. He looked round and smiled.

'Haven't seen your face in here before,' she said. 'New in town?'

'Yes. Just . . . just passing through.' Harry, against his better judgement, edged closer to her. She was older than she had first appeared: crow's feet round her eyes were inexpertly disguised by thick make-up, and great black swathes of mascara sought to enhance her small, sad eyes. The roots of her strawberry blonde hair were the same colour as the mascara, as were her high-heeled shoes and ill-advised mini-skirt. Harry forced a smile. This, he thought, was the first woman he had been close to for months. The thought made him feel slightly sick.

'All on your own?'

'Yeah.'

'So where's your missus?' she teased.

Harry felt even more sick. 'I haven't got one,' he mumbled. The woman smiled knowingly. 'No? You look like a married man.'

This was positively painful for Harry, but he was, he reminded himself, on a job. 'I was,' he replied tersely.

At his words the woman's blank expression changed and her face became softer. Hardened as she had forced herself to become, she sensed, nevertheless, a sadness about Harry. And she saw that her words had caused him distress. In an awkward but genuinely felt gesture, she placed her hand on his for a moment. 'I'm sorry,' she said.

Harry smiled. 'That's the way it goes.'

The moment passed. The woman, mindful that she, too, had work to do, smiled at him in a grotesque parody of flirtation. 'Brighton,' she whispered, 'is a lonely town when you're on your own.'

Harry couldn't stand it any more. He pulled his hand abruptly away and eyed her dispassionately. 'I'm looking for a woman called Pamela Hewitt,' he said. 'Do you know her?'

His companion looked at him in disgust. Then, without a word, she walked away.

'Shit!' said Harry under his breath. Then he turned morosely back to the bar and downed the rest of his whisky in one. I didn't, he thought, handle that at all well.

It wasn't, in the circumstances, altogether surprising. Harry was still reeling from wounds deeper than those of either Tony or Maureen. They had lost their jobs: Harry had simultaneously lost both his job and his wife.

Joyce's death had not been unexpected, but its inevitability hadn't eased the pain. She had tried to tell him that her dying would be a release for both of them: for her it would mark the end of her terrible, painful and futile battle against terminal cancer, and for him the end of agonised months as an impotent spectator.

But her death, when it had come, had been quite different. Joyce, unable to stand the pain and the helplessness that had enveloped both of them, had committed suicide – and Harry had watched her die. That fact and that memory was one he would carry alone for the rest of his days. He had returned home to find Joyce, empty pill-bottles beside her, on the verge of unconsciousness. Horrified, he had reached for the telephone to call an ambulance, but Joyce, her voice feeble yet her words urgent, had stopped him. He would never forget her final, desperately sad yet deeply dignified speech.

'Please, Harry,' she had said. 'Let me die this way. It's what I want. I'm a wreck; I'm so tired. At least this way I'm in control of something.' And then she had looked deep into his eyes and asked him if he understood.

He had understood. He understood that she was tired of fighting a battle she could never hope to win; a battle that was, day by day, robbing her of both her body and her spirit. He understood that, this way, Joyce would be able to preserve the one thing left to her – her dignity. So he had cradled her in his arms, told her that he loved her, and then held her until her eyes closed for the last time and her breathing grew fainter until, finally, it stopped.

Hours later he had called for a doctor who pronounced Joyce dead but regretted that he would be unable to issue a death certificate because, while it looked like suicide, he couldn't rule out what he euphemistically called 'other causes'. Harry had expected that; he had realised that there were discrepancies between the time of his arrival home, the time of Joyce's death, and the time he had called the doctor. The 'other causes' were, of course, murder.

Harry knew they would never be able to pin a charge of murder on him: he also knew that they wouldn't want to. Everyone knew Joyce had been terminally ill and everybody, from the medics to his colleagues on the force, viewed her suicide as a welcome release. But Harry had reckoned without

David Graves. In a twist of bitter irony, Harry, as a policeman under suspicion of wrongdoing, was questioned at CIB by his ex-Guv'nor. Gravesie's ability to antagonise Harry was surpassed only by the unwavering accuracy of the barbed remarks with which he had so successfully nettled Tony Clark beyond endurance. Graves hadn't really suspected Harry of murdering his own wife; what he had really wanted to know was where Harry had been before returning home to discover Joyce's body. He had been, had he not, on holiday? On specially granted leave in order to look after his ailing wife? Harry knew that, sooner or later, Graves would find out where he had been; would discover that not only had he been out of the house for a few days but that he had been out of the country.

Harry had been in Tunisia with Tony Clark, helping his ex-boss on what had turned out to be the first contract of Tony Clark Associates. He hadn't wanted to go, but Joyce had been adamant. She had been the one to persuade Tony to take her husband away with him, to get him away from her for a few days. She had joked that she wanted Harry out of the house for a bit because having him constantly at her side was 'cramping her style'. The truth of the matter was, of course, that she wanted to take her overdose in private and die in peace. It had been Harry's tragedy that he had returned sooner than expected.

Graves's line of questioning had been spectacularly unsubtle. Harry remembered sitting opposite him and wanting to punch him, very hard, in the mouth. Graves was his junior by at least ten years and was a graduate of the 'rules and orders above all else' school of thought. After several minutes of questioning, Harry had finally realised that there was no future for him in the force if he had to call people like Graves 'sir'. So he had risen to his feet and obeyed his first instincts: he punched Graves, very hard, in the mouth. And then, like his wife before him, he took the only dignified option left to him. He resigned.

Tony and Maureen had saved him from drinking himself to death. Tony had taken him under his wing and helped him through the first, awful weeks and then, without either of them formally discussing it, Harry had helped Tony on another job and found himself as an unofficial 'associate' of Tony Clark.

Dragging his thoughts back to the present, Harry deposited his empty glass on the grimy bar and walked hurriedly out of the Sailor's Arms. The highly expensive whisky had done little to alleviate his spirits after his depressing encounter with the prostitute. Not only had she brought back bad memories, she had done nothing to help him with the task in hand – the finding of Pamela Hewitt. He hoped Mo had had more success.

Two hours later he almost regretted Mo's success. While she hadn't located Pamela, she had established that she had a pimp who frequented a pub called the Mariner. The nautical name should have been enough to set alarm bells ringing in Harry's mind. It was even seedier than the Sailor's Arms, and the pimp, Kenny Bates, had been nasty,- violent and unco-operative. When Harry and

Maureen had walked into the pub and questioned him persistently about Pamela, he had led them outside and, in a practised manner, pulled a knife on them. But he had reckoned without their police training. In three seconds flat Harry had had him in a half-nelson up against a parked car and Maureen had the knife. And then, just as Kenny decided that divulging information about Pamela was probably a good idea after all, four men had walked up to them with the air, and doubtless the intention, of joining in the fight. Maureen, in a flash of inspiration, had pulled her bus pass on them and yelled, 'Police! Move along, please.'

'Well,' she said later to Harry, 'it was *nearly* true.'

It was also effective. The four men had walked on, and Kenny Bates had talked. And now, as they walked towards Maureen's hotel, they had a companion – Pamela Hewitt. She looked, unsurprisingly, not dissimilar to the prostitute at the Sailor's Arms, yet she was younger and her face had a gentleness that seemed at odds with her calling.

She smiled brightly at Harry and Maureen as they entered Mo's room. A strange couple, she thought. Still, they said Kenny had sent them, and who was she to argue with Kenny? Threesomes, however, were not really her thing. Her smile hid her unease. 'This feels kinky,' she said brightly. 'I don't usually do threesomes, but if Kenny said—'

'Kenny,' interrupted Harry as he walked to the mini-bar in search of a less expensive whisky, 'is a louse. You've got yourself a right one there.'

Pamela looked sharply at him. It was an odd comment, she thought, for a punter to make, yet she couldn't help agreeing. 'I know,' she replied. 'Tell me about it.'

'No, Pamela,' said Maureen. 'It's you who's going to be doing the telling.'

Suddenly fear visited Pamela's face. 'Hey, what is this?' She looked from one to the other as realisation dawned. These two were the Fuzz. She could usually tell them a mile off. Why on earth had she failed with this couple? 'You're coppers, aren't you?' she asked belligerently. 'What the hell d'you think you're doing? Why have you brought me here?' She stood up and lunged for the door. Maureen, none too gently, put a restraining hand on her arm.

'Cool it, Pam,' replied Harry. 'We're not coppers. We were, but now we're on our own.'

'On your own?'

'Yes,' said Mo. 'Freelance security consultants.'

'Security consultants?' Pamela looked blank. 'What would security consultants want with me?'

'You met,' said Maureen without preamble, 'some Irishmen here in Brighton two years ago. Before the shootings outside the Grand Hotel. That's right, isn't it?'

Whatever question Pamela had expected, it certainly wasn't that one. She tried to hide her astonishment. Then she stuck her chin in the air. 'Might be. Might not be.'

Maureen was unimpressed. 'Look, Pamela, we're here on business. OK, so it's not the business you thought it was, but I'd have thought that would be a relief to you—'

'Just like it's a relief,' interrupted Harry, 'to know that this business pays you as well.'

Maureen glared at Harry. He smiled back.

'How much?' asked Pamela.

'It depends on whether or not you met any Irishmen before the shootings.'

Pamela looked at Maureen. The question, she felt, was harmless enough. It was also a line of questioning that held, for her, a personal interest. She shrugged. 'Yeah, well I met one Irishman.'

'Was he one of the terrorists who was shot by the SAS?'

'No. But I did see one of them. Seamus Kelly. He had his face in the paper afterwards.'

'Where did you see him?'

'He was with Danny.' Pamela's voice softened as she spoke the name. 'The Irishman I knew.'

'Danny?'

Pamela looked at Maureen and her eyes took on a dreamy, faraway look. 'Danny McLaughlin. He was really nice. He had this lovely Irish voice, you know. And,' she added, 'he was rich.'

'And you saw Seamus Kelly with Danny McLaughlin?'

'Yeah. A night or two before the shootings.'

'And where,' asked Harry cautiously, 'is McLaughlin now?'

Pamela bowed her head. 'I dunno. He disappeared after the shootings. I never saw him again.'

Harry and Maureen exchanged a brief, pointed look. Mo infused her voice with gentleness as she asked Pamela if she had known him well. Either she had, thought Mo, or she wished she had.

'I thought,' said Pamela, 'I thought . . . that it was something different with him. I saw him for three weeks. He said he was here on business. Then . . . then he just pissed off.' She stopped and then added, succinctly and with feeling, 'Bastard.'

'Was his business with Seamus Kelly?' asked Harry.

'I don't know. I didn't know who Kelly was until afterwards. I asked Danny who he was, but he accused me of spying on him.'

Maureen rose from her chair and went to sit beside Pamela on the bed. 'What did you tell the police about Danny?'

'The police?'

'You were questioned after the shootings, weren't you?'

'I didn't tell them about Danny. I didn't want to get him into trouble. And you tell the police as little as possible, right?' She looked at Maureen and grinned as she realised what she had said.

'You didn't,' continued Maureen, 'think that Danny might have been involved with something?'

'I didn't really know much about him.'

'But if he'd had business with Kelly,' said Harry, 'he'd have had a reason for disappearing. He might've been responsible for their deaths.'

Pamela looked horrified. 'But he couldn't have killed them! It was the Army did that, wasn't it? Not Danny.'

Neither Mo nor Harry replied. 'Do you know,' asked Maureen after a moment, 'where we could find Danny?'

Pamela looked miserably at her. 'I wish I did.'

Maureen sighed and looked at Harry. She

41

wondered if he was thinking the same thing as she was. Trying to locate a man who had last been seen in Brighton two years ago would not be easy – and it would get more difficult by the minute. Up against TV deadlines as they were, Mo couldn't ask Sarah Teale for more time to locate Danny McLaughlin. But she could ask for more manpower.

4

'Sarah.' Maureen smiled and then turned to her companion. 'This is Tony Clark. Tony, Sarah Teale.'

Sarah got up from her desk and looked appraisingly at Tony. She liked what she saw. He looked, she thought, like a man who was comfortable with himself. Perhaps too comfortable, though. The piercing blue eyes stared unashamedly into her own and his handshake, like his demeanour, was firm and confident and, she conceded, pleasing.

Tony too liked what he saw. The blonde hair, the easy smile and the air of self-assurance all appealed to him. But she would, he mused, be no pushover. This one was used to getting her own way.

'I'd like Tony,' continued Maureen, 'to help me out. We used to work together.'

Sarah turned and smiled mischievously at Mo. 'They used to say that Polish police always went round in threes. One who could read, one who could write, and' – here she turned back to Tony – 'one to watch over the two intellectuals.'

Maureen stifled a giggle as she caught the

expression on Tony's face. For a man with many abilities, he singularly lacked the capacity to laugh at himself: especially when the joke was made by a woman who was younger, good-looking and, as was the case on this job, who was calling the shots. Tony masked his initial frown with a small and unconvincing smile as Sarah motioned for them to sit down. Had she known that Tony's air of breezy self-confidence had been achieved at no small cost, she might not have made that flippant remark.

When Harry and Maureen had returned from Brighton that morning, they had headed straight for Tony's flat and had found him rumpled, unshaven and still in a dressing-gown. Enforced idleness didn't suit him and the lack of phone calls to Tony Clark Associates had enforced, of late, much idleness. To while away the hours Tony had taken, like Harry after Joyce's death, to attacking the whisky bottle. And the empty whisky bottle, accompanied by an empty carton from the Chinese takeaway, had been the first thing Maureen had noticed on entering the flat. Tony, unable to explain away his hangover and dishevelled state with tales of a wild night out, had greeted them somewhat sheepishly. His mood had improved immeasurably when Mo had explained that she wanted him on board to help find Danny McLaughlin, yet at the back of his mind a small voice told him that, if he needed a reminder that his life had altered dramatically and not necessarily for the better, then this was it. A few months ago he would have been the one in control; Mo and Harry would, while on duty, both have been calling him 'Guv'. Now they were descending on him to find him at his worst, and to offer him employment. While he couldn't conceal his delight at being involved, he still felt that things were the wrong way round. But as he went off to shave and dress, he reflected that he was in no position to refuse Mo's offer. Then, as he combed his hair, donned a highly flattering blue linen suit and a bright pink tie, he grinned at his image in the mirror. Maureen, he told himself, might be in charge on this one, but surely it was an indication that Tony Clark Associates would soon be in business with, as in the good old days, the three of them?

On his return to the sitting-room Maureen, as if reading his thoughts, had firmly quashed that idea. 'I don't want you to think,' she had said, 'that this is setting the pace for the future. You and Harry are only helping me out because the job's got too big for one person.' Tony and Harry had looked at each other, a look that spoke volumes.

But now, settling himself uncomfortably opposite Sarah Teale, Tony was beginning to wonder how on earth he was going to adapt to this new situation; to being an employee of Maureen's – and being ultimately answerable to this young and, he now thought, impossibly arrogant woman.

Sarah turned to Maureen. 'Did you find the prostitute?'

'Yeah. She was involved with a man she knew as Danny McLaughlin. We think he was Seamus Kelly's contact. According to Pamela Hewitt he met Kelly just before the shootings, then disappeared.'

Sarah's face brightened. 'So he was IRA?'

'We assume so.'

'But that's fantastic! If he was Kelly's contact, we've *got* to find him.' She smiled at Maureen and then reached for the file on her desk. 'I think the next move has to be Seamus Kelly's widow.' She picked up a pen and scribbled something on a yellow Post-it note. Then she tore off the note and, still without a glance at Tony, handed it to Maureen. 'This is her address in Kilburn. Maybe she'll be able to shed some light on who and where this McLaughlin is.'

Tony, almost squirming with the indignity of being ignored, couldn't bear to keep quiet any longer. He was also beginning to think that Sarah Teale was not just arrogant, but naive as well. He leaned forward in his chair and smiled at her. 'Er, with respect . . . we don't know what we're dealing with here. If McLaughlin is IRA, even supposing we do find him, I don't think he'd be very forthcoming.'

Sarah looked at him in annoyance. 'I'm making a programme about the SAS shootings in Brighton, and if McLaughlin was Kelly's contact, I need him.' Then, satisfied that she'd dealt with his impertinent interruption, she turned to Maureen again.

But Tony was riled. 'Oh, fine,' he countered as he leaned back and crossed his legs. 'We'll just look him up in the phone book, then.'

Sarah didn't reply at first. Then, with quiet deliberation, she looked at the source of this sarcastic outburst. 'I'm sorry, what was your name again?'

Tony glared at her. 'Tony Clark.'

Sarah made a pyramid with her arms and

rested her chin on her hands. 'Do you believe, Tony, in rule of law?'

'Do I what?'

'Or do you believe in extra-judicial executions on the streets of Britain?'

'No. But then I don't believe in letting bombs go off, either.'

Sarah looked down her nose at him. 'What bomb? The van that Kelly drove into Brighton might have been loaded with Semtex, but there were no detonators found either in the van or in Ryan's car.'

Tony shrugged as if that were a mere irrelevance. 'They were IRA, and now they're dead. No documentary is going to bring them back.' He learned forward again and looked at her as if she were a young, and not to bright child. 'What are you alleging anyway? That the SAS kill people? You might as well allege that the police wear blue serge.'

'Tony—'

Sarah silenced Maureen with an imperious hand and glared at Tony. 'My programme isn't biased in favour of the IRA. I find their actions repellent. But I also find it very worrying that MI5 and the SAS can run around blowing people's heads off without any kind of public inquiry.'

Tony looked coolly back. 'I do actually have some experience of the security services, Ms Teale, and I also know a bit about terrorists. And just to sit here in your ionised office making programmes about shoot-to-kill strikes me as very naive.'

Maureen could hardly believe his cheek. She turned to him and put a restraining hand on his

47

arm. 'Tony, for God's sake . . .' But Sarah, her face now slightly flushed in anger, was as unstoppable as Tony. 'I know quite a bit myself, Mr Clark. Since I started work on this series, I've discovered quite a few things.' She indicated the telephone beside her. '*That*, for instance, is bugged.' Then she got to her feet and looked dismissively at him. 'But then this is all quite irrelevant. If you're not up to finding McLaughlin, then perhaps Maureen can find someone who is.' With that she addressed Maureen. 'I've got lunch with a junior minister from the Home Office. If there's anything more to get out of the prostitute, I think I ought to come down to Brighton with you, see what she'd be like on camera.' Then she smiled briefly at the embarrassed Maureen, shot one final acrimonious glance at Tony, and walked out of the room.

Maureen broke the ensuing uneasy silence. With feeling, she turned to Tony and, slowly enunciating the words, said, 'Well Bloody Done, Tony.'

Tony had the grace to look abashed. 'Well, I mean, for God's sake . . .'

Maureen stood up. 'For God's sake nothing! You've done your damnedest to lose me this job!'

'But I haven't, have I?' Tony too rose from his chair. 'She still wants you to find this guy. I mean, Christ, what a ludicrous—'

'Ludicrous is she? I happen to think she's bloody smart. She's prepared to stick her neck out and she's one of the few people I've ever met who . . .' Maureen faltered as she noticed the expression on Tony's face. She'd seen that expression before when she'd voiced admiration for another woman. Tony, she reckoned, considered admiration as synonymous with – or perhaps a substitute for – foreplay, and she wasn't going to get into that particular argument. Instead, she took a deep breath and, with rather more force than was necessary, stuck the Post-it note to the front of Tony's suit. 'Why don't you,' she said, 'go and exercise your colossal charm on Seamus Kelly's widow?'

Tony, aware that he had overstepped the mark with Sarah, took Harry with him to Kilburn. Mary Kelly, he mused, might be cast in the same mould as Sarah Teale and he couldn't afford to antagonise her. Nor could he bear the indignity of being taken off the case – a case in which he was beginning to get extremely interested. The more he had learned about it, the more he smelled the signs of a cover-up; the tell-tale signs of the big boys' rules of which he had fallen foul. From what Mo had said, Special Branch were being extremely helpful, and Tony was intrigued by that helpfulness. To him, it smacked of dissent in the security services; of Special Branch, outraged that they had been superseded by MI5 and the Cabinet Office, pointing an accusatory finger. And Danny McLaughlin was the only person who would know exactly where that finger was ultimately pointing.

The other reason why Tony took Harry with him to Mary Kelly's was because he wanted to know the outcome of the meeting from which Harry had just returned. While Tony and Mo had been at the offices of Encounter Productions, Harry had met the man for whom he had once worked: the man who had long been a thorn in the side of Tony Clark.

The man was the man whom Mo suspected of putting Encounter Productions on to her. He was John Deakin, ex-Special Branch and ex-chief superintendent of CIB. As far as many people were concerned, he should also have been an ex-, or perhaps current, convict.

A year ago, in what had been the most spectacular case of Tony's career, he, Harry and Mo had investigated a conspiracy which had spiralled upwards and finally led them to its source – their boss, John Deakin. Tony, who had always hated Deakin, had barely been able to contain his euphoria when, one memorable day, he had arrested him. He remembered the exact words he had used as he had snapped handcuffs round Deakin's wrists and announced, 'John Deakin, you are under arrest for conspiracy to commit burglary, dishonestly handling stolen goods, suspicion of conspiracy to pervert the course of justice and suspicion of conspiracy to commit murder.'

The euphoria had been short-lived. Deakin had known that Tony would have a great deal of difficulty in proving his case. Furthermore, and far more importantly, Deakin had friends in high places who were more interested in his numerous contacts and experience in security than in any criminal activities in which he might have been involved. So John Deakin, to Tony's everlasting outrage, had walked away from the Old Bailey a free man. True, he had also walked away as an ex-policeman, but that hadn't, it seemed, harmed his career. In no time he had ensconced himself in a plush suite of offices in a discreet corner of Westminster and, even more discreetly, acted as a freelance consultant for the security services. Later, he had also walked back into Tony's life, and, ironically had been instrumental in perpetrating the disastrous and dramatic end of Tony's own career in CIB. To add insult to injury, he had caused Tony to lose a woman he had truly loved. But the final irony was that, of the three cases Tony had thus far investigated in his new incarnation as a security consultant, two of them had come to him through Deakin. It seemed that he would never be able to rid himself of the man: he hated him, yet he needed him. It was a situation that suited John Deakin very well. Harry, in the days before CIB, had worked under Deakin at Special Branch, and he alone of the trio maintained some sort of respect for him. Tony wanted to hit him every time he saw him. At least, he thought wryly as they drove to Kilburn, he hadn't hit Sarah Teale.

'Deakin,' mumbled Harry as he lit his umpteenth cigarette of the day, 'says he's never heard of Danny McLaughlin. Seemed surprised when I told him what we were working on.'

'In other words, he didn't tip Special Branch to contact Sarah Teale and then push her in our direction?'

'In Mo's direction, you mean.' Harry grinned as he corrected his ex-Guv'nor.

'Yeah. In Mo's direction.' Tony, tight-lipped, concentrated on the road ahead. 'So,' he added, 'Deakin doesn't know what Branch are up to?'

'Seems not.'

'Hmm.'

'But,' added Harry, 'he wasn't convinced that

51

McLaughlin is IRA.'

'Interesting. Why?'

''Cos there's no indication of IRA involvement at all. The three dead men were *described* in the press as IRA, but there were no salutes fired over their coffins.'

'How very interesting that Deakin still remembers that after two years,' said Tony. 'But I'd rather,' he added, 'hear it from the widow herself.'

The widow of Seamus Kelly swore blind that her husband had never been involved with the IRA. She claimed she had no idea how her husband had got involved or why he was murdered. Neither had she ever heard of a man called Danny McLaughlin. And as Tony persisted with his questioning, her eyes blazed out of her worn, weary face, and she told him that if she knew who had set up Seamus, she would kill him with her own bare hands. Then she shrugged in resignation and added sarcastically that she'd have a hard job doing that, wouldn't she? One lonely Irish widow against a Government and an Army didn't stand much of a chance, did she?

As she ushered them to the door of her shabby, run-down maisonette, she wished them luck in finding Danny McLaughlin, whoever and wherever he was. She reckoned that the people who found him would cause more than a little embarrassment 'up high'.

Mary Kelly – not to mention Tony Clark and Harry Naylor – would have been more than a little interested in two meetings that were taking place elsewhere in London. Both of them yielded more information than their own, and both corroborated Mary Kelly's last statement.

The first was at an outdoor venue, the architecturally derided South Bank Centre, which housed London's National Theatre, the Hayward Gallery and the Royal Festival Hall. To most people, Londoners and tourists alike, the complex – once you had got over its concrete ugliness – served as a meeting, eating and drinking place as well as a cultural haven and, with its superb location on the banks of the Thames, a vantage-point from which to view many of London's most famous landmarks. Two of the nearby buildings, however, remained anonymous, and their occupants preferred to keep things that way. One was the headquarters of MI5, the other of MI6, and one of the two men casually strolling along the riverbank had just left the former building.

He turned to his companion and reflected, as Tony Clark had done many times, that John Deakin possessed an uncanny ability to be well informed about almost everything concerned with state security.

'There's a documentary series being made,' Deakin was saying. 'Suggestions of a shoot-to-kill policy.' He paused and looked the other man directly in the eye. 'The name Danny McLaughlin has cropped up.'

'Has it, indeed?'

Deakin ignored the look of near-amusement. 'I made some inquiries at Branch. Drew a blank.'

'No surprises there.'

'I thought,' persisted Deakin, 'that maybe you could enlighten me?'

The man from MI5 paused before replying, almost regretfully, 'Er, no can do, I'm afraid.'

'You don't know of him?' Deakin didn't believe that for a moment.

His companion stopped and turned to face him. 'John, to all intents and purposes, McLaughlin has ceased to exist. We'd prefer,' he added, 'to keep it that way.'

Deakin was silent for a moment, taking in the subtext of what he had just heard. 'Do I take that as meaning,' he asked eventually, 'that whoever finds him becomes an embarrassment?' The man from MI5 looked across the river towards the blank edifice of the MI6 building. Then he turned and looked pointedly at his own headquarters. And finally, his gaze swept the concrete maze of the South Bank complex. 'Too many warrens and dark corners around here,' he said. 'Time we moved on, don't you think?'

The other meeting took place in altogether less mysterious circumstances. Sarah Teale, sitting in a Jermyn Street restaurant and sipping a fragrant, chilled glass of Chablis, was fast recovering her composure after her encounter with Tony Clark. The man opposite her, she had to concede, had much to do with her escalating spirits.

Jeremy Taylor was a Home Office minister destined – according to a few well-timed press releases written by none other than himself – to go places. He certainly possessed the qualities essential to a politician on the rise. His charm was undeniable; his looks were appealing to old ladies and young women alike, and he was always well but not over-dressed. He was also a brilliant orator and a highly accomplished liar. Yet he wasn't lying to Sarah Teale. He rather enjoyed telling her the truth and, when they had first met at a party two years before on the terrace of the House of Commons, he had told her the truth about his instantaneous attraction to her. Sarah had laughed and deflected his advances with ease, but deliberately without conviction. She, on the brink of becoming a producer at that point, knew what a valuable contact someone like Jeremy Taylor could prove to be if she played her cards right.

Jeremy Taylor himself, well aware of the power of television and the potential of friendly producers, had been thinking along the same lines. So, by mutual and tacit agreement, they had developed a friendship that contained, for old time's sake, a small amount of flirtation, and a large amount of exchanges of information. Sex, they both privately thought, was not and never would be on the agenda. The unmarried Sarah was not attracted to pompous men, and Jeremy, with his wife safely tucked away in Northumberland, was now enjoying a passionate affair with a secretary who looked not unlike Sarah, but who was thankfully blessed with a much smaller brain.

Over the Chablis and lightly steamed monkfish, Jeremy was admonishing Sarah over her shoot-to-kill series. Had his own party not been in power, he would happily – and anonymously – have supplied her with any amount of information that could damage the Government. And, more importantly, he had his own career to think about.

'As far as Her Majesty's Government is concerned,' he said in the pompous manner which Sarah had almost grown to regard with affection, 'the timing of your documentary could be a little more felicitous.' Then, twisting his fingers round the stem of his wine glass, he looked over its rim and added, with gentle irony, 'but that's the price of freedom of speech, isn't it?'

Sarah laughed. She knew there was no such thing as freedom of speech when the Government wanted to cover up something really important. 'It's only one programme of a series, Jeremy. We're not just examining dirty tricks and shoot-to-kill against Irish Republicans. Our scope is much wider than that. One of the programmes, for instance, is about Chile.' This time it was her turn to give him a gently mocking look. 'And your Government has nothing to hide where Chile is concerned, does it?'

'Indeed not.' Jeremy looked slyly at Sarah. Was the mention of Chile, he wondered, just a coincidence, or had Sarah got wind of something? Nobody in the media could possibly know about the current and highly secret negotiations between Chile and Britain to develop jointly what some people referred to as 'non-perishable goods' and other people knew to be military equipment. No, he decided, Sarah was just teasing. Chile had enough nasties in its past for her to concentrate on. It certainly had more than its fair share of what Sarah called shoot-to-kill policies. 'Shoot-to-kill?' asked Jeremy, nimbly side-stepping South

America. 'It's a bit of a cliché, don't you think?' He laughed. 'Bit like "Phew, What a Scorcher!" '

Sarah, however, didn't laugh. She leaned further across the table. 'So you're telling me that the British Government has never authorised a clandestine shoot-to-kill policy?'

Jeremy paused for consideration. If he didn't tell her, someone else would. And he knew and trusted her well enough to be sure that this particular conversation was strictly off the record. Then he spread his hands eloquently in front of him and answered her question. 'Can you name me one country which hasn't?'

Sarah, astonished by the frankness of his admission, opened her mouth to reply, but Jeremy was already in full flow, and getting carried away by his own wit. 'Well,' he added, 'maybe Iceland hasn't, but then they've only got trolls to worry about.' Sensing that Sarah wasn't in the mood for appreciating his little jokes, he leaned forward and, urgently and earnestly, started justifying the policy of shoot-to-kill. 'We have fanatics, killers, bombers, you name it. Of *course* we've had shoot-to-kill. How else do you expect us to deal with these people?'

Sarah was flabbergasted. 'You're saying,' she almost whispered, 'that the law doesn't apply to everyone?'

Jeremy leaned back and gestured dismissively. 'Oh, in an ideal world, perhaps. But the beauty of the SAS is that they kill the people you want dead without your having to tell them to. Privatise them and you've got the best Rentokil in the business.' He leaned closer to Sarah again. 'Most of us in

Government have fantasies about Sass and Five that border on the sexual. Don't you?'

Sarah wasn't entirely sure that he was joking. There was a gleam in his eye that she hadn't seen before. As she watched him nonchalantly sip his wine, she felt suddenly revolted. 'You are telling me, then – you are openly admitting – that the Government wanted Ryan, Fitzpatrick and Kelly to be executed in broad daylight?'

Jeremy smiled at her. 'What I'm saying, Sarah, strictly *entre nous*, is that I was far happier seeing those three blown away than I would have been climbing into my Brighton hotel bed with a nice hot parliamentary researcher, only to experience the earth moving for all the wrong reasons.'

Sarah would have giggled had not the import of his words been so serious. 'But,' she said, 'there's been no acknowledgement that "those three" were IRA. Sinn Fein has repeatedly denied that they had anything to do with them. And,' she added, 'there was no IRA salute fired over their coffins.'

'My,' said Jeremy tartly, 'you *are* well informed.'

'I'm even better informed after this little chat.'

Jeremy looked evenly at her. 'Now, Sarah, you know the rules. This conversation has been completely off record. But,' he dabbed smugly at his lips with a pristine linen napkin, 'in exchange for what you heard – or rather, *overheard* – from a Government minister who shall remain anonymous, you will of course film me for your programme?'

Sarah nodded. That had been part of their deal. 'Do you want me to go over the questions I'll be asking you?'

Jeremy smiled. 'I don't really think that will be necessary. There's only one important answer, isn't there?'

'Is there?'

'Oh, come on, Sarah. All you want to get from me on film is my response – the Government's response – to the existence of a shoot-to-kill policy. And do be sure to film my best profile while I vehemently deny that there is any such thing.' Then, with a pleased and almost predatory smile, he stabbed the remaining morsel of monkfish and licked his lips.

5

Mo was feeling pleased with herself when she returned home that evening. It was good to be working again, and it was even better to be in charge. She smiled to herself as she savoured the words 'in charge'. It wasn't that she got a kick from being in control, it was more that the situation was new to her and she was enjoying it far more than she had anticipated. Apart, that was, from Tony. She pursed her lips and stamped on the accelerator as she cast her mind back to the meeting with Tony and Sarah. If there was one thing that would make Sarah think Maureen wasn't up to the job, it was her insistence on bringing in Tony. 'Bloody Clark,' she said out loud. She knew him well enough to realise that his first impression of Sarah had been favourable – and favourable to Tony meant that he was convinced she would fall for him. Well, she hadn't. Quite the reverse. It had been patently obvious that Sarah considered Tony to be arrogant, chauvinistic, opinionated and stupid.

Maureen grinned. The first three adjectives were, she knew, accurate. But Tony was anything but stupid. Mo frowned as she considered the other adjective that, especially of late, she would use to describe him. Insecure. Sarah would no doubt be surprised to hear that, but Maureen had no intention of telling her. 'Oh by the way,' she imagined herself saying, 'do excuse Tony's rudeness – he really doesn't mean it. It's just that he's had a hard life, what with a messy divorce, a girlfriend who committed suicide on him, an ex-boss who is an unconvicted criminal and who comes back to haunt him and, oh yes, the accusations of murder that led to his dismissal while on a case that was, in fact, engineered by the married woman with whom he was having an affair and who just happened to be a senior MI5 officer . . .' Mo sighed. No, Tony's past was not something Sarah would want to know about. It sounded, anyway, like something out of a thriller.

But Mo knew there had been nothing thrilling about the awful events that had finally led to the end of his affair with Angela Barrett, the woman from MI5. Mo had always disliked her and had been puzzled by Tony's complete infatuation with her. She was, Mo considered, a great deal older than Tony; she was married to an important barrister and had two grown-up children. Why on earth had Tony fallen for her? Mo shrugged in answer to her own question. Love, she supposed, was blind. And love, she knew, had stopped Tony from trying to expose MI5 when he found out they had been playing nasty little games with other people's lives. He would, in any case, never have succeeded in blackening MI5's reputation, but he would, in the process of trying, have made a fine mess of Angela's life. The big boys had made sure of that with their compromising photographs and video of Tony and Angela in bed together. And one of those big boys had been John Deakin.

Mo compressed her lips in distaste. Where there was MI5, there was, invariably, John Deakin in the background. And where there was John Deakin, you could be sure Special Branch was lurking in the wings. Now, as she sped through Shepherd's Bush, she felt a horrible sense of *déja vu* about the current investigation into the Brighton shootings.

She tried to dismiss her forebodings as she turned into Starfield Road and searched in vain for a parking space near the house she and Kate had bought together only a few months previously. One thing she did not wish to discuss with Kate was the possibility of her being involved, yet again, with the duplicitous, dangerous dealings of the security services. Thus far, Kate had kept to herself her doubts about Mo's employment with Encounter Productions. She didn't want to undermine Mo's still shaky confidence, but Mo knew full well that Kate was worried about the way things were going. Finally finding a parking space, she locked her car and walked to the house. She stopped for a moment and studied it from outside. It was a typical London Victorian terraced house, unremarkable from outside, but spectacular inside. It had been a deliberate policy to buy a house which hadn't yet been modernised so that she and Kate could run riot with their interior-design schemes. And thus far, thought Mo, they had succeeded. They had knocked down most of the ground-floor walls, making a large, light and airy living-space with stripped floors and a few, well-chosen pieces of furniture. They had gutted the kitchen at the back, added a conservatory that gave on to the small but exquisite garden, and now they were in the process of renovating the upstairs. But renovations cost money, and while Kate had urged Mo not to worry about that after her dismissal from 'the job', Mo was very concerned about her lack of funds. The last thing she wanted to be was a kept woman.

'Hi!' she yelled as she let herself in. 'Anyone at home?' Stupid question, she thought. There wasn't likely to be just 'anyone' – there would only be Kate.

'Be with you in a minute!' came the reply from upstairs. Mo, a strange expression on her face, stood motionless in the open hallway for a full thirty seconds before making her way through to the kitchen. She made a bee-line for the fridge and smiled when she found an unopened bottle of wine on the top shelf. She paused for a moment, reflecting that she was probably drinking too much. Then she shrugged, grabbed the bottle and rummaged in a drawer for a corkscrew. Drink, she excused herself feebly, was a hazard of a job. It failed to register in her head that, technically speaking, she didn't have a job any more. This investigation was just a freelance contract, a one-off.

Two minutes later Kate came downstairs and stopped, as yet unseen by Maureen, at the kitchen door. She frowned as she took in the sight of Mo, a bottle by her side, already halfway through her first glass of wine. This, she thought, was a familiar sight. It was a sight that had often greeted her in the days when Mo was still at CIB, exhausted after a full day of chasing round London with Tony Clark and Harry Naylor. So much for her fervent hope that those days were firmly in the past.

Then Mo saw her and smiled. 'Drink?' She waved at the bottle and indicated a second glass.

'No thanks.' Kate looked instead at the kettle. 'I think I'll have a cup of tea instead.'

Maureen shrugged. 'Please yourself.'

'How did it go?' asked Kate conversationally.

'What?'

'The meeting with the production company.'

'Oh God.' Mo grimaced. 'A disaster. Tony and Sarah got on like a house on fire. Literally. You could hear the sound of windows imploding as they talked. Or argued, I should say.'

'Tony?' Kate hadn't expected that. 'Tony Clark? Is he in on this?'

Mo moodily cradled the glass in both hands. "Fraid so. Oh God!' she added, 'that reminds me. I've got to phone Harry.' Heading for the phone on the other side of the room, she missed the expression on Kate's face.

'So,' said Kate quietly, 'it's just like old times?'

Maureen, in the middle of dialling, missed the undertones of her remark. 'No,' she replied. 'This time I'm the boss, but Tony's being a pratt and he's lousing up my chances of working for Sarah again.' Then, as the phone at the other end was answered, she spoke into the mouthpiece. 'Harry? Hi, it's Mo. Listen, can you ring the Grand Hotel in Brighton and find out if they've got any records of McLaughlin staying there? Yes, I know it's a long shot, but we don't have much to go on.' She listened for a moment and then spoke again. 'Yes, Tony told me about Kelly's widow.' Then, after listening again, she nodded her head and added, 'Yeah, pretend you're McLaughlin and you need a new receipt for tax purposes. Thanks.'

As she hung up, Kate turned to face her and, as casually as she could, asked Mo what Sarah Teale was like. At the mention of Sarah's name, Mo's face brightened and she beamed at Kate. 'Sarah,' she said, 'is great. No messing.'

Kate's worries about the 'old team' being back in business and Maureen's relationship with Sarah Teale were intensified when, later in the evening, the phone rang as she and Mo were watching television. At first, hearing Mo talking, Kate assumed the caller was phoning for a friendly chat. But her ears pricked up when she heard Mo's unenthusiastic 'Does it have to be tonight?'. Then she stiffened as Mo's voice took on a more positive tone and she finished the conversation with the words, 'OK, OK, I'll be there.'

Kate pretended to be glued to the television as Mo hung up, turned round and sighed. 'That,' she said, 'was the prostitute.'

'The Brighton one?'

'Yep.'

'Oh. Are you going down to see her?'

"Fraid so. She says she's got news about Danny McLaughlin.'

But Kate wasn't interested in Danny McLaughlin. 'When will you be back?'

Mo looked at Kate for a moment and then

reached once more for the phone. 'I don't know,' she replied as she dialled, 'I think that'll depend on Sarah. She'll want to come with me.' On the sofa, Kate clenched her fists until her knuckles went white.

The conversation between Sarah and Mo, as they drove towards Brighton, was in marked contrast to Mo's stilted dialogue with the uncharacter-istically truculent Kate. As they chatted, Mo felt as if she had known Sarah for years. They were totally at ease with each other as they talked, often changing the subject without apology in the manner of old friends. But Mo was nonplussed when Sarah, completely out of the blue, asked her if she knew anything about Chile.

'Chile?' Mo looked round in astonishment. 'No, not really. Why?'

'Oh, no reason really. Just the look on my junior minister's face when I mentioned that I wanted to do a documentary on it.'

'He must've been quite gratified you were doing something on Chile,' said Mo. 'Much less close to the bone than Brighton.'

'Well . . .' Sarah faltered and then decided she could trust Maureen enough with what little infor-mation she had. 'That's the official line, anyway.'

'Meaning?'

'Meaning that a little bird told me that the Government, despite its public horror at Chile's stance on human rights, is negotiating arms deals with them.'

'That won't make them very popular if it leaks out.'

'Quite.' Sarah looked at Mo and smiled. Mo smiled back.

'But how,' asked Mo after a moment's contemplation, 'would that tie in with a documentary on shoot-to-kill policies?'

'It wouldn't be anything to do with the shoot-to-kill series,' replied Sarah. 'It's just an idea floating round my head at the moment. It seems like a good opportunity to expose hypocrisy at a high level.' She grinned. 'Again.'

'Christ, Sarah! You really relish playing with fire, don't you?'

Sarah chose silence as the best form of assent. Nobody could, she knew, accuse her of being unadventurous.

At her mention of fire, Mo remembered her remark to Kate about Sarah and Tony getting on like a house ablaze. 'By the way,' she said, 'I feel I ought to apologise for Tony's behaviour at the meeting. He really shouldn't have said what he did.' Apologise if you must, she cautioned herself, but never explain. 'I don't know,' she finished lamely, 'what got into him.'

Sarah just laughed. 'Don't worry about it. The mouth's usually a few steps ahead of the brain in cases like that. How long were you working with him?' she added.

Maureen noted the 'with'. She made a mental note not to let slip the fact that she had actually been working *for* Tony. Sarah would be horrified. 'Three years,' she said.

Sarah winced. 'Must have driven you up the wall.'

'Mmm. We had our moments.'

'Poor you.' Then, suddenly feeling a need to study her fingernails, she added, 'But I suppose I should feel sorry for his wife.'

Maureen hadn't expected that one. She looked curiously at her companion. 'No wife. Not any more.'

Sarah raised her eyebrows in a mocking gesture. 'Oh? Too many young WPCs chasing that cute arse of his?'

So that, thought Mo, is the way the land lies.

Back in London, Kate was also wondering how the land lay, and she was beginning to let her thoughts torture her. She knew and accepted that Maureen always became distracted and offhand when she was on a job and under stress, yet she sensed something different about her behaviour this time. Something she had never seen before. Then she herself was distracted by the shrill tone of the telephone. She smiled in relief. At least Mo was keeping her informed of her movements.

But it wasn't Mo. It was Tony Clark. A rather pissed Tony Clark. He wanted, he slurred down the line, to discuss something important with Mo.

'Well, you can't,' snapped Kate. 'She's not here.'

'Oh. When'll she be back?'

'I don't know. She's gone to Brighton.'

'Brighton?'

'That's what I said.'

'Oh. To shee the prozzie?'

'Yes.' Kate had no intention of telling Tony that she hadn't gone alone.

'S'all right, then, I suppose,' mumbled Tony down the line.

'What?' Kate sighed in exasperation. 'Are you drunk, Tony? You're not making much sense.'

'No no. I'm abs'lutely fine. T'rrific.'

'Good. I'll tell her you called.'

'Kate?'

'What?'

'Are *you* all right? You sound . . . you sound . . .'

'I'm just tired, Tony. Goodnight and sleep well. You sound like you need it.'

At the other end of the line, Tony looked in surprise at the handset he was holding. He hadn't expected Kate to hang up so quickly. He tried, and failed, to replace it and then weaved back into the main room of the pub where Harry, in a similar state, was lolling against the bar.

'Not there,' said Tony.

'Oh.'

'Got Kate. Sounded annoyed. Dunno why.'

Harry closed one eye and tried to focus on the glass in front of him. 'Maybe . . . maybe Kate feels we're to blame for Mo losing her job and getting into bed with us.'

At the mention of bed Tony perked up and remembered the reason for his phone call to Mo, the important information he'd wanted from her. 'Who else,' he asked Harry as one elbow slipped off the bar, 'd'you think might know Sarah Teale's home phone number?'

6

Pamela Hewitt was being followed. In her line of work this wasn't exactly unusual, but this time there was something sinister about her pursuer. He had been following her, at a distance, ever since Maureen Connell and Harry Naylor had questioned her about the shootings. And now Pamela was scared. Two years ago, she had thought of Danny McLaughlin as her passport to a life of respectability; he had been kind to her, he had been the first man to treat her as a woman rather than as a body, and he had promised to take her out of her life of prostitution. Then he had disappeared. Pamela had taken a long time to get over him and to come to terms with the fact that he was like every other man who had ever entered her life: a user.

But she had never paused to consider that McLaughlin might have been a member of the IRA. She took few moral stances in her life, but terrorism was the one thing she couldn't abide. And the ex-policemen who had questioned her had raised the possibility that Danny was a terrorist. She still didn't believe that: terrorists were animals. Danny might have been a user, but he hadn't been evil. Yet she did think that he had been more than he'd appeared. She believed that he was the key to a mystery which Maureen Connell and Harry Naylor wanted to solve.

Not that Pamela cared very much about the mystery. She did, however, care very much about her own life, and now she believed it was in danger. She was being followed and watched and she was scared.

It didn't take her long to work out that her follower was stalking her because he thought she knew the whereabouts of Danny McLaughlin. There could, she reckoned, be no other reason for following Pamela Hewitt. And it was a perfectly valid reason, because Pamela Hewitt *did* know the whereabouts of Danny McLaughlin.

She had lied to Maureen and Harry mainly out of pride. She didn't want them to find him because she didn't want to know the reason why he had disappeared, why he had broken all his promises to her. And then, after they had left with entreaties from Maureen to contact her if she remembered anything, Pamela realised that she possessed information that might be valuable. Suddenly she didn't want it any more. She didn't want to be followed by some sinister, unknown and possibly dangerous man. She reasoned that if she gave that information to Maureen Connell, then she, not Pamela, would be followed. So, having made up her mind, she had phoned Maureen.

But now, in the seedy anonymous hotel room to which she had directed Maureen over the phone, she was getting cold feet. She hadn't reckoned on the bossy blonde with the tape-recorder accompanying Maureen. She was damned if she was going to be recorded or filmed and get herself into even more trouble. She was buggered if she was going to be part of some dodgy TV programme about terrorism and shooting. She had, in short, changed her mind.

Faced with Pamela's recalcitrance, Sarah Teale decided that her journalistic fervour was in danger of jeopardising the entire investigation. Maureen, not she, was the one Pamela had trusted enough to phone; the one she seemed to want to confide in. And now Sarah, blundering in with her tape-recorder, had frightened her. She nodded to Maureen and motioned her outside.

In the cramped corridor, she whispered urgently, 'Look, she obviously won't talk with me here and I think we're in danger of frightening her off.' She smiled apologetically. 'My fault, sorry.' Then, looking at her watch, she added, 'D'you think you could stay? All night if necessary?'

Maureen nodded. 'Sure. Probably best that way. Maybe if she sleeps on it she'll think again in the morning. What'll you do?'

Sarah grinned again. 'Get the train back to London. Serves me right for being a fool rushing in, I guess. Anyway, it was daft of me to come. I've got an edit first thing.' She turned to leave, gesturing at Pamela's door as she did so. 'You'll let me know, won't you, the minute she comes up with anything?'

Again Maureen nodded. Her mind was elsewhere: it was on the phone call she would have to make to Kate telling her she was about to spend the

72

night with a prostitute. She hoped Kate would be able to see the funny side. Maureen eyed the nasty little corridor and cheap plywood doors with distaste. She herself wouldn't be doing much laughing if she had to spend the night here.

Not only did she end up spending the night, she had to endure most of the next morning as well before Pamela decided to talk – mainly because Pamela didn't get up until midday. It was, she said in token apology, a habit you got into in her line of work.

Mo suggested a walk along Brighton beach and then a spot of lunch. Pamela, looking furtively around her as they left the hotel, agreed reluctantly. She didn't particularly want to go outside, but nor did she want anyone else to overhear what she was going to tell Maureen.

'You said,' prompted Maureen gently, 'that you were being followed. Do you know who by?'

'No,' said Pamela succinctly. 'Maybe I was wrong.'

'Well, if it's any comfort,' continued Maureen, 'we're not being followed at the moment. Believe me. I've been followed. I've done the following. I know what it's all about.'

'Why'd you leave the Filth?' asked Pamela suddenly.

Mo grinned. It was a long time since anybody had associated her with filth. 'Difference with my boss,' she said, not altogether untruthfully.

'So why're you working for a TV company?'

Maureen knew the answer to that one. She had already used it on PC Barrett, the man who had led her to Pamela. 'Well, I won't be working for them

73

for much longer,' she replied with a wry smile, 'unless you tell me why you phoned me last night.' That decided Pamela. She was beginning to like Maureen and didn't want her to lose her job. And if Maureen started getting followed by strange men . . . well, that was part of that job, wasn't it? 'Look,' she said, 'I did lie to you. A bit. Danny said he wanted to move to somewhere quiet. He promised he'd write to me. He never did.' Maureen bit her lip. Was this all she had on McLaughlin? That he'd gone 'somewhere quiet'? 'But,' continued Pamela, 'I know where he is.'

'You do? Where?' This was much better than she had expected.

'A place called New End Farm, Minstead.'

Maureen had already extracted her notebook and hastily wrote down the address. 'How did you find that out?'

Pamela looked slightly sheepish. 'Someone rang up. I listened in, on the extension in the loo. It was,' she added as if in explanation, 'the only time we did it in his room.'

'Oh.' Maureen didn't have a reply for that one. 'And that,' she said after a moment, 'was two years ago? At the time of the shootings? You don't know if he's still there?'

'No,' said Pamela bleakly. 'But if he is, will you tell him . . . will you tell him, no hard feelings?'

Pamela's profession did not generally lend itself to lunch invitations, and she wasn't going to let Maureen renege on her offer of a free meal. Mo, quelling her reluctance and her desire to get on with tracking down Danny McLaughlin, was obliged to fulfil her part of the bargain, and so didn't manage to contact Sarah until after their meal.

Sarah, on the other hand, was frequently asked out to lunch. Today, tired after her fruitless journey to Brighton and a morning's edit fraught with problems, she would have cancelled the last-minute invitation she had received but for the fact that it came from an unexpected, not to say intriguing quarter. It came from Tony Clark.

At thirty-five, Sarah had invested most of her adult life in her career and, although she had not admitted as much to herself, was now feeling that there must be more to life than material success and job satisfaction. Her colleagues and even, grudgingly, her rivals, admitted that she had ample of both. Ambition had been something instilled into her from an early age. Sarah was a London girl born and bred. Her mother and father – a teacher and a lawyer respectively – had been aware of their elder daughter's potential and had encouraged her from the start. That encouragement had, Sarah knew full well, as much to do with her own abilities as with the misfortunes of her siblings. Her elder sister, Amanda – the 'beauty of the family' as relatives had so tactlessly repeated in front of a gawky adolescent Sarah – had dropped out of school aged fifteen and, a year later, dropped out of circulation altogether. Another year went by while her parents tried everything in their power to track down their errant daughter. Eventually they succeeded: Amanda was found living in a sordid squat with a boyfriend who lived up to his nickname – 'Septic'.

One look at Amanda's emaciated frame and haunted eyes had been enough to inform her parents of her lifestyle. They lost no time in checking their daughter into a drug rehabilitation clinic. Now, nearly twenty years later, Amanda was on her fifth attempt at drying out. Drink, drugs, casual sex and an appalling diet had taken their toll on her once glorious looks and Sarah's sister was now a shadow of her former self. She was also bitter at life and insanely jealous of Sarah, claiming that her younger sister had always been her parents' favourite. Everybody else, of course, knew better, and Sarah herself, even at the age of fifteen, when she had first been exposed to Amanda's way of life, had realised that the danger – if not the blame – lay with people like the revolting Septic. In an unguarded moment, Amanda had confided to Sarah that Septic had forced her on to the streets when money for drugs had run low. And the look in Septic's eyes when the Teales had taken Amanda away had chilled Sarah to the bone. He had remained silent throughout the whole hysterical procedure, but his expression had spoken volumes. Amanda, it intimated, was just one fish in the sea: there would be many more impressionable, malleable middle-class girls for him to seduce, corrupt, use and abuse.

Sarah often wondered if Amanda's experiences had been instrumental in making her choose investigative journalism as a career. Certainly the desire to root out and expose evil and injustice had been with her from an early age, and the saga of Amanda had undoubtedly put her on the path towards justice and truth. But it was the fate of her brother, David, that had really set the wheels of Sarah's career in motion. The Teales had had high hopes for David. Sarah's father, especially, had been immensely proud of his charming, sporting and highly extrovert son. While not academically brilliant, David had secured a place at Durham University through his rugby prowess, and had been looking forward to three years of parties, girls, games and, less enthusiastically, the odd lecture. And then, three weeks before he had been due to go to Durham, he had been knocked down in the street by a speeding driver who had shattered both his legs and his dreams.

David never went to Durham; instead he spent the next eighteen months trying, in vain, to walk again. Sarah still shed tears about what might have been. David, however, was more stoic about what life had handed him. Now married with two children and a career in computing he was, he repeatedly assured his family, extremely happy. But he was, and always would be, wheelchair-bound, and his lingering bitterness was evident every time sport came on the television. Tight-lipped, David would reach for the remote control and switch channels while his family pretended they didn't notice what was happening.

The accident had been bad enough, but its immediate repercussions, as far as Sarah and her family were concerned, were far worse. The man who had destroyed part of David's life and all of his aspirations hadn't been prosecuted. He hadn't even been brought to trial. There had been, to the Teale's family's horror, an 'inquiry' into the incident. An eyewitness who seemingly materialised from nowhere claimed that David had walked straight into the path of the vehicle and the doctor who had operated on him in hospital had verified that David had been 'intoxicated' at the time. David had repeatedly insisted that, to a healthy eighteen-year-old prop forward, three pints of bitter hardly constituted intoxication, but to little avail. The case was closed with unseemly haste. As there was no prosecution, there were no damages awarded, but David, two months later, had been given an astoundingly large grant from a foundation that looked after the well-being of promising athletes cut down in their prime. The entire affair reeked of a cover-up, but all the Teale family's attempts to see justice done had met with official brush-offs. David, the implication ran, should count himself lucky to be both alive and rich.

By the time of David's accident, Sarah was already at film school. And by the time it became evident that the driver was not even going to be brought to trial, Sarah had decided that, while cameras never lied, the people you pointed them at most certainly did. She quickly developed an ability, while still learning her craft, to ask the most pointed questions and watch her interviewees squirm as they realised – usually too late – that she had put them right on the spot and that there was no escape. The driving force behind her first interviews had been her ardent wish that the person in front of the camera had been the man who had mown down her brother and escaped scot-free.

Sarah's professionalism was soon noted and, even before she graduated, the job offers started pouring in. After that, she had never looked back careerwise. Yet in the rare, dark and private moments when she stopped to consider what she had achieved, she wondered if it had all been worth the effort. While she conceded that she was naturally ambitious, an extra onus and a greater pressure had been provided by her parents. Sarah was 'the lucky one': no misfortunes had befallen her; she would, they knew, rise to the top of her profession. And Sarah herself felt she owed them that. They had, with infinite patience and sympathy, rearranged their lives to cater for David and Amanda. But Sarah was the strong one, the capable one, the one who was going to make it on her own. How, then, could she ever complain to them that life, for her, also had its difficult moments? The answer was, she couldn't. Every time she saw them, she radiated happiness and confidence. Every time she changed job, her colleagues marvelled at her brisk efficiency and calm determination. All her acquaintances agreed, privately, that Sarah was far more interested in her career than in personal relationships. None of them knew that, just as privately, Sarah had doubts. While she loved her work, she also liked to play, and there hadn't, for longer than she cared to recognize, been anybody to play with.

Her last relationship had begun in a frenzied flurry of passion and ended so disastrously that she had, for over a year now, been wary of involving herself with any man beyond superficial flirtation. Sam had been – and still was, for all she knew and cared – a sound recordist. They had met at the wrap party for a series on which they had both worked and the attraction had been both mutual and instantaneous. It had been, of course, purely sexual, and, Sarah realised now that she could view it from a safe and objective distance, had been doomed from the start.

Sam had loved sex, but he hadn't loved Sarah. He loved her beautiful flat in Butler's Wharf, her myriad of contacts in the media and elsewhere, her successful friends – and the fact that to be attached to Sarah Teale would do no harm whatsoever to his own stagnating career. Sarah was so busy at work that it was several months before she clicked that Sam's enthusiasm for her flat ran to using it to entertain his own, hardly successful, yet very young and usually extremely pretty friends. Only gradually did it dawn on her that she was the accidental recipient of far too many phone calls for Sam from far too many young girls.

And then one memorable night Sarah had returned from work unexpectedly to find Sam in bed – in *her* bed – with one of his young and pretty friends. What had made the situation infinitely worse was that this particular friend happened to be male.

Sarah, mainly because she was so used to being the calm, cool and collected one both with her family and at work, rarely lost her temper. But on the few occasions she did, she went completely berserk. She had been so completely out of control with Sam that he had left, hot on the heels of his little friend, and without half his clothes. Sarah had derived enormous pleasure from weighing down the forgotten items with every cheap and nasty trinket Sam had ever given her and hurling the bundle over the balcony into the Thames. It had sunk without trace and she hoped that, like Sam, it would never resurface.

The episode had left her with a new and particularly disconcerting form of self-doubt. Never before had she had to question her looks or her feminine appeal. But because of Sam, she found herself wondering if she, as a person rather than as an object, had any appeal at all. And then she had ducked the issue altogether by throwing herself even deeper into her work and avoiding situations where she would meet single men and, infinitely worse, parties orchestrated by friends who were becoming increasingly concerned by her single status.

If there was any consolation after the discovery of Sam's unconventional sexuality, it was that Sarah found herself, strangely, more tolerant of other women. She had always preferred the company of men to that of women until the débâcle with Sam. After that she found herself increasingly drawn to the company of women, although definitely in a non-sexual way. It was an irony not lost on her that the woman whose company she was now enjoying immensely was, she had learned, gay. Maureen, as was her way, had made no bones about that fact when they had chatted en route to Brighton.

Perhaps, thought Sarah as she brought her mind back to the present and the intriguing lunch invitation, making friends with Maureen had had an effect that she was only just beginning to appreciate. Mo's openness, her forthright manner and lack of the boring social retraints that characterised so many of Sarah's London friends had

made Sarah drop her guard a little. Without being
intrusive, Mo had somehow managed to penetrate
beyond the barriers that Sarah was only dimly
aware of having erected around herself. And,
while those barriers were down, Tony Clark had
sauntered into her office and caught Sarah Teale
as she really was. He had found her as she really
was and that, she reflected ruefully, was probably
why he had annoyed her so much. When he had
walked into her office, she had, even before he had
opened his mouth, formed an immediate impression. She had thought him good-looking, and,
from the thin yet firm line of his lips, arrogant and
possibly dangerous. After he had opened his
mouth she had revised her opinion and decided
that he was a complete pratt: a plod who had made
detective only because he was a man, a fast talker,
and probably a bully. She had been surprised that
Maureen had chosen to get him on board. Yet,
after their meeting, and rather to her annoyance,
the image of Tony Clark refused to go away. There
was something about him. She had tried to convince herself that it was his high irritation factor.
Afterwards, and even more to her annoyance, she
had been forced to concede that it was his eyes.
Well, not exactly his eyes, but the way they had
looked into hers. Or maybe, she reflected, it was his
body. Most of the men she had been out with had,
for some reason, been slight. Tony, under what
she told herself was a slightly too sharp suit,
seemed to be very well built. Then she cursed
herself for fantasising like a schoolgirl and, to her
even greater annoyance, found herself behaving
like one. For no reason at all, and when she was still

quite alone, she blushed. She had also been on her own when Tony had phoned her and invited her to lunch. That had given her a moment or two's privacy for reflection after she had hung up: a moment or two to collect her thoughts and tell herself that she was being an idiot and that he had only phoned because he was, after all, working for her.

She arrived ten minutes late at the Soho restaurant Tony had booked and was glad to see that he was already there. She was also glad to see that he was looking somewhat morose. That would be, she reckoned, because of his guilt at yesterday's behaviour. She was not to know that he was still nursing a hangover from last night's episode with Harry and that his sad expression was due to the fact that he was lost in contemplation of the frequently made decision that he would never, ever, drink again.

He looked up, and then stood up as Sarah approached the table. Her quick, confident smile matched her step as she went up to him and shook his proffered hand. 'Apologies,' she said.

'That's my line,' grinned Tony. 'Bad morning?'

Sarah sat down and wearily ran a hand through her hair. Tony liked the way she did that. It made her look more human, more vulnerable than she had yesterday. 'Yes,' she replied. 'I went down to Brighton last night, didn't get much sleep, and then my edit started late.' And then, she might have added, I spent rather too long in the loo checking my already perfect make-up. God knows why, she thought as she looked closely at Tony and revised her opinion of yesterday. He doesn't look

83

nearly so good today. Older. Baggy round the eyes. He was also, at the mention of where she had been last night, looking alarmed. 'Brighton? With Mo?'

'Yes.'

Tony looked at her. Well, he thought, so that's the way the land lies. What a bloody waste of time. He beckoned to a passing waiter. 'What'll you have to drink?' he asked her.

'Oh, just a mineral water.'

'And I,' said Tony, 'will have a Bloody Mary. A large one.' Without another word, he passed Sarah a menu and looked down intently at his own.

Sarah, slightly puzzled by the sudden change in his behaviour, leaned towards him. 'Tony, I know my phone is tapped, but I don't see why we can't have a little chat in my office. Cloak-and-dagger stuff is for overgrown schoolboys.'

Fifteen-love, thought Tony. Then he remembered the colossal charm he had used on Mary Kelly. He smiled. 'Just being informal. What I really wanted to say,' he added almost conspiratorially, 'is that . . . well, we didn't get off to a very good start, did we?'

Sarah grinned and leaned back in her chair. 'But you *did* go to see Mary Kelly. That's a start, isn't it? Tell me about it.'

She already knew about it: Mo had phoned her with Harry's report about what they had found out – or rather hadn't found out – from Seamus Kelly's widow. But she wanted to hear it from Tony himself. And as she listened she decided that he wasn't a pratt after all, that he did have nice eyes, and that his lean but muscular frame looked better

84

in today's leather jacket than in yesterday's sharp suit.

As he talked, Tony decided that Sarah wasn't quite so brittle as she had first appeared and was, in fact, a great deal of fun. And, now that they were no longer fighting each other, he found her forthright, questioning manner a pleasant challenge rather than an irritant. As they mulled over the missing Danny McLaughlin, Sarah suddenly looked up at him. 'We might,' she said, 'be missing something here. MI5 ran the anti-terrorist operation in Brighton, but nothing they knew about Kelly et al ever reached Special Branch.'

'So?'

Sarah leaned forward. 'So if McLaughlin was Kelly's contact, who's to say he was IRA? He might,' she added pointedly, 'have been MI5.'

'You mean he might have been an informant?'

'Well, Sinn Fein's press spokesman insists that those three weren't IRA. They've continually denied it, but no one cares. As far as everyone's concerned, the whole thing's neatly tied up.'

Tony looked at her. 'Not everyone. Special Branch have been extremely helpful to you.'

Sarah returned his gaze. 'And so has Mo.' She paused. 'And are you still going to help?'

'Absolutely.'

At that point they were interrupted by a sound that was becoming increasingly familiar in London restaurants – the 'beep-beep' of a mobile telephone. Tony instinctively reached into his breast pocket, thinking that the sound was his own bleeper, calling him back to duty at CIB. It was with horror and not a little embarrassment that he

85

realised he no longer had a bleeper, nor a job with CIB. Sarah, thankfully, hadn't noticed what he was doing – she was too busy fishing in her handbag for the source of the interruption. With a half-apologetic smile at Tony, she switched her phone to 'talk' and cradled it between ear and chin.

'Hello. Sarah Teale.' Then her face lit up at the sound of the voice on the other end. 'Maureen!'

Opposite her, Tony glowered.

'You talked to her? Brilliant . . . No, it's just the background noise. I'm in a restaurant having lunch with Tony. What? . . . Yeah, OK, I'll pass you on to him.' She smiled and handed the phone to Tony. 'Maureen,' she said unnecessarily.

Tony took the mobile. 'Hello, Mo? . . . Yeah, we've just been comparing notes.' Then, as he listened to Mo his eyes lit up and his hand delved into his pocket for a pen. Looking up at Sarah, he gestured feverishly for something to write on. Smiling, she tore out a page from her Filofax and handed it to him. 'OK,' he continued, 'fire away.' As Mo spoke, he wrote down an address on the paper and then frowned. 'I've to tell him *what*? No hard feelings?' He shrugged. 'Sure. I'll get on to it right now. It's the only thing we have to go on.'

Then he switched off the mobile and handed it back to Sarah with a triumphant smile. 'She's found out where he is!'

'McLaughlin?'

'The same.'

'But that's brilliant! Good old Mo.'

Tony stood up. 'And good old Tony's going to go down there.'

'What? Now? Where?'

'Yes. The New Forest.'

Sarah looked worriedly at him. 'But we don't actually know for sure whose side he's on.'

'Exactly. That's why I'm going.'

Doubt mingled with concern crossed Sarah's features. 'Well . . . look after yourself.'

Tony grinned down at her. 'Don't worry. I always do.'

As he hurried out of the restaurant, Sarah's worry increased. He shouldn't, she thought, be going alone. Then she shook her head in annoyance as she remembered that he was an ex-cop and, more importantly, currently her employee. Of course he should be going.

'Would you care for coffee, madam?' said a voice at her shoulder, 'or just the bill?'

Startled, Sarah looked up. The waiter's friendly smile disguised his suspicion that this couple were about to do a runner. He'd seen that ruse many times before. Usually the woman, feigning horror that she was still holding her boyfriend's telephone, rushed after him, never to be seen again. 'Oh,' said Sarah. 'No. No coffee, thanks. Just the bill.' Then she smiled ruefully at the empty seat opposite her. Well, she thought, he may not be arrogant after all, but he sure ain't gallant. I thought he was taking *me* to lunch.

7

Tony was relieved on two counts: that he'd established a friendly rapport with Sarah and, more urgently and perhaps more importantly, that he was finally seeing some action. Irrespective of whether or not Sarah was actually more interested in Mo than in himself, she was technically his employer and as such it was in his interests to be seen to be working. It was also in his interests that Sarah revise her initial opinion of him. He reckoned he'd succeeded there. Furthermore, it was exhilarating to be working alongside Mo and Harry again. Just, in fact, like old times. He conveniently neglected to remind himself that, strictly speaking, he was working for, not with Mo. That, after all, was only a minor detail.

It took him nearly two hours to reach the New Forest. Central London's traffic had been predictably grim and the A3 more crowded than he anticipated. Minstead, when he found it, was a small, unremarkable-looking village in the middle of nowhere and New End Farm, judging by the appalling pot-holed and seemingly endless drive that led towards it, was at the end of the world. It also had the air of being deserted. No vehicles were parked outside the decrepit farmhouse, and the place certainly didn't appear to be a working farm. Realising that, were anybody guarding the place, his arrival would already have been noted, he parked right outside the front door and jumped out of the car. A shiver ran down his spine. There was *something*, he felt, something not quite right about the place. It was too eerie, too quiet. Shrugging and chiding himself for being fanciful, he went up to the door and knocked loudly. No reply. He knocked again and then peered through the grimy window. Still no reply. Then, at first tentatively and then more loudly, he called out. 'Mr McLaughlin? Danny? Hello?'

Still the silence prevailed. Sighing, Tony walked round the side of the farmhouse, looking through windows as he went. Although the place was furnished, he could see little in the way of personal effects. At the back of the farmhouse, he saw a pair of French windows, leading to what was obviously a sitting-room. After a quick, furtive glance around him he tried the latch. It gave easily under his touch and two seconds later he was inside the house.

The sitting-room, at least, showed signs of habitation. There was a large TV, several magazines scattered around and, on the table in the centre of the room, a half-empty cup of coffee. A cup that, as he reached for it, was cold to the touch. He looked around again. On another table near the door he noticed a telephone. Treading lightly, he crossed the room, picked it up, listened, then nodded to himself as he heard the dialling tone. Then he went to the door, listened more carefully and quietly opened it.

As he peered into the hallway he could hear his heart pounding. It was the only sound that disturbed the oppressive, spooky atmosphere of the place. Directly opposite him was an open door leading towards the kitchen. After a quick look inside he established that no one was there. And now, he thought without enthusiasm, for upstairs. He gulped – a noise that seemed even louder than his heartbeat – and put a tentative foot on the first stair. It creaked loudly. So did the next one, and the next.

By the time he reached the landing his nerve-ends were screaming and Tony Clark, veteran of fifteen years in the force, was on edge. Too late he realised that his enthusiasm to find McLaughlin had overtaken his better judgement. Why hadn't he brought Harry with him? Why hadn't he waited for Mo to get back from Brighton? What on earth was the hurry? Well, he thought as he pushed open the first door on his right, there *was* a hurry. He was no longer in the police force; he was a free-lance security consultant working to a deadline – a TV deadline.

But had he not paused to consider the finer points of why he happened to be alone in an isolated farmhouse in the middle of nowhere, he might not, one minute later, have found himself lying flat on his stomach praying for his life.

'Lie down!' commanded the voice behind him. Tony turned round to find that the voice meant business. The man standing in the corner of the room was holding a shotgun, and it was aimed, in an expert manner, at the back of his head. 'Who are you?'

'I'm Tony Clark,' he stammered. 'I'm with a TV company.'

'So what are you doing in my house?' The Irish accent was unmistakable.

Tony tried to turn his face away from the foul-smelling carpet and, in what he hoped was an even voice, replied that he had been sent to talk; that he was a researcher. Then he sensed, rather than heard, the man approaching him. Lying prone on the floor, there was little he could do to stop himself being searched. The man, efficiently practised in his moves, searched his pockets, extracted his keys, his wallet and, finally, Sarah Teale's business card. Then he retreated to the unmade single bed that constituted the sole item of furniture in the room, and lit a cigarette. The gesture was casual, but Tony, straining to see from his undignified position on the floor, noted that the gun was still pointing at his head.

'Who sent you?' barked his attacker.

'My producer, Sarah Teale. The number,' he added, 'is on the card.'

The man looked at the card. 'Why?'

'We're making a documentary.'

The man was silent for a moment. 'How did . . . how did you find this place?'

'Pamela said you'd be here. Pamela Hewitt from Brighton.' Tony wished he had a better view of the man's face. The sharp intake of breath told him he was on the right track.

'Pamela? What does she want?'

'To send her love.'

The man was silent for a moment. Then, in a totally different voice – one that betrayed more than a hint of emotion – he asked, 'What's she looking like these days?'

Tony cursed silently. He, out of the three of them, was the only one who hadn't met Pamela. Then his mind raced back his hurried phone conversation with Mo. 'She's looking OK,' he said. 'And,' he added pointedly, 'she wants you to know that there are no hard feelings.'

From the intake of breath from the man on the bed, Tony reckoned he'd passed the test. And when, a moment later, the man told him to get up, he knew he had.

Once on his feet, Tony looked at the man. The shotgun was now lying beside the bed, and the man's half-smoked cigarette dangled from his lips. Although he was still seated on the bed, Tony judged that he was short and stocky, with a shock of dark, curly hair and piercing green eyes. If his accent hadn't betrayed him as Irish, his looks certainly did the trick.

Tony, mustering all the dignity he could find after his ignominious spell on the floor, brushed down his jeans and leather jacket and looked dispassionately at the man. 'You are, I take it, Danny McLaughlin?'

Instead of answering, the man rose from the bed and took a last drag of his cigarette. Then, after exhaling with a sigh that Tony could have sworn was relief, he motioned for Tony to follow. Any reluctance Tony may have had to do so was offset by the fact that the shotgun remained by the foot of the bed. He followed.

The man led him down the stairs, through the sitting-room and out the French windows to what passed as the garden. Once out in the open, he smiled apologetically and explained, 'It's safer out here.'

'Ah,' was all Tony said.

After walking together for a few yards in uneasy silence, McLaughlin asked Tony why he had come to Minstead.

'To ask you,' said Tony concisely, 'about the Brighton shootings two years ago.'

'What makes you think I had anything to do with that?'

Tony looked at him. 'Pamela Hewitt said she saw you with Seamus Kelly a couple of days before three men were shot.' When McLaughlin didn't reply, he added, 'We also know the SAS seemed very well informed of their whereabouts.'

Still McLaughlin didn't reply.

'Were you,' persisted Tony, 'Kelly's IRA handler?'

Obviously still undecided, McLaughlin stared at Tony. Then, appearing to make up his mind, he smiled wryly. 'That,' he said, 'is what Kelly thought I was.' Smiling another humourless smile, he continued, 'And Five weren't about to disabuse him.'

Tony couldn't help registering his complete surprise at that disingenuous reply. So Sarah had been right after all. 'You mean you're an inform-ant for Five? Were *any* of you IRA?'

'Fitzpatrick was. But then he didn't know that Brighton was an unofficial operation; didn't know it wasn't sanctioned by the IRA.'

'What about Ryan and Kelly?'

McLaughlin sounded weary as he replied, 'No. They were just sympathisers. Kelly was a romantic. They'd shot a friend of his in the Murph. He thought ... he thought he was making a gesture.'

Tony looked at the man with ill-concealed distaste. 'You set up three innocent people to be shot by the SAS?'

'Something like that,' mumbled McLaughlin.

'That's not,' replied Tony coldly, 'the role of an informant.'

McLaughlin stopped in his tracks and looked Tony in the eye. 'I never knew they would get killed. That wasn't the deal. What d'you think I'm doing,' he added quietly, 'living here? I refused to do any more for MI5 after that.'

Tony too stopped. Here, he thought, was the clincher for Sarah's programme. 'Are you prepared,' he asked, 'to say that on camera?' When McLaughlin didn't reply, he added, 'They could hardly bump you off once you'd gone public.'

McLaughlin didn't answer immediately, and Tony, aware of the import of his question, didn't press him. Finally, McLaughlin spoke. 'If I came clean on camera,' he said, 'you'd have to get me some money and somewhere to live until the programme came out.'

'You reckon,' said Tony quietly, 'they're still keeping tabs on you?'

McLaughlin gestured futilely around him; at the distant farmhouse, and at the countryside that had been his prison for two years. 'I don't know. I really don't know if they're bugging this place or not.' Then, looking helplessly at Tony, he added, 'I don't know who I am or what I'm doing any more.'

Tony acted quickly. This was not an opportunity he was going to pass up and he wanted to get the ball rolling before McLaughlin had a chance to change his mind. Leaving the farmhouse as soon as they got back from their walk, he instructed McLaughlin to wait, and on no account to leave the house, until he returned. Tony had no intention of losing his man as soon as he had found him.

Sarah, when he phoned her from the local pub, was ecstatic. Without McLaughlin, her programme, and especially her interview with the anonymous Special Branch officer, would raise a few hackles in the corridors of power. But with McLaughlin, it would be dynamite. It would, she knew, make the headlines for days or possibly weeks, and it would certainly lead to a public inquiry into the conduct of the security services, and of MI5 in particular. She had, therefore, no compunction about providing McLaughlin with a safe haven until the programme was transmitted. This was going to be the highlight of her career.

It was also, reflected Tony as he made plans to transport McLaughlin to London, going to do his own career no harm. It would make Tony Clark Associates a force to be reckoned with and earn him a reputation as a highly reliable and productive operator. He also hoped it would make Maureen see the light and bring her on board once and for all. With visions of a new office with a neat, discreet nameplate, computers and a fax machine, he reckoned the bad times were over once and for all.

He had, however, reckoned without McLaughlin's paranoia. The man refused to go to London in daylight, and he also refused to go in Tony's car. He insisted, instead, that they hitch a lift.

'*Hitch*?' Tony was dumbfounded. He hadn't hitched-hiked since he was a teenager, but still remembered with distaste the long, wet and lonely nights he had spent by deserted roads waiting in vain for someone to take pity on him.

'Yes,' said McLaughlin. 'Hitch. We drive to the main road, dump your car and then we hitch.'

'Er . . . why?'

McLaughlin looked at him. 'I don't know what your programme's dug up,' he said quietly, 'but you can bet your bottom dollar that Five's taking a very close interest. Even if they no longer see me as a threat, they're sure as hell going to be worried about what you and your Miss Teale are up to. Now, do we hitch or not?'

'Yeah,' said Tony with a resigned shrug of his shoulders. 'We hitch.' What had Sarah said about cloak-and-dagger games being for little boys? Still, he wasn't going to argue with McLaughlin, and Sarah, judging by her unconcealed excitement on the phone, was evidently prepared to do anything he requested. Tony hoped the man didn't have his sights set on staying at the Ritz until the shoot-to-kill programme came out.

They waited until it was dark and then, in uneasy silence, they drove away from the isolated farmhouse. McLaughlin, unsurprisingly, seemed morose. He had spent two years at the farm, remaining resolutely silent about the Brighton killings, and wondering who had and who had not forgotten about him. For Danny McLaughlin was not just of interest to MI5: even though the three men he had unintentionally led to their deaths were only sympathisers, the IRA, he had never forgotten, had good reason to be extremely displeased with him.

It was Tony who broke the silence with a question that had been bothering him for some time. 'Why did Five,' he asked, 'set up those three men when sooner or later someone was going to realise it was a hoax? That they weren't IRA?'

McLaughlin looked at him as if he had not yet graduated from kindergarten. He grinned sourly as he answered. 'Because it's war! And I'm not talking about terrorism. I'm talking about Branch, Five, Six, all plotting against each other.' He gesticulated wildly, and with disgust. 'Turf battles! That's what they're fighting. The great propaganda piss-take. Look,' he added more calmly, 'Five wanted publicity. Wanted to make Special Branch look like a bunch of tossers. I was told to engineer an incident.' He shrugged. 'High profile. Political points. And it wasn't just the Government that came out smelling of roses.'

Tony didn't reply. McLaughlin's statement corroborated what he knew of the anonymous Special Branch officer's interview with Sarah. MI5 had been running the show at Brighton, and MI5 was unaccountable. Nobody was going to ask any embarrassing questions. But then nobody, presumably, had thought that two years later, an inquisitive TV journalist might come along and mess things up. And nobody would have suspected that Tony Clark might find Danny McLaughlin. Suddenly Tony began to appreciate the man's paranoia.

McLaughlin's voice suddenly interrupted his thoughts. 'Turn off the road.'

'What? Here?'

'Yes. There's a dirt track down on the right. We'll leave the car there and walk through the woods to the main road. When we hit it, you flag down a vehicle. And don't, for God's sake, go for a car. I'll keep out of sight till you've got the lift.'

Tony shot a sideways, irritated glance at his companion as they bumped down the dirt track. This, he thought, was something he was going to have to get used to. Detective Superintendent Tony Clark did not let people speak to him that way. But Detective Superintendent Tony Clark no longer existed. Tony was now a freelance, and freelances, when their mission was at stake, did exactly what they were told. Again, he wished he'd brought Harry with him and that he hadn't rushed off with such alacrity in pursuit of Danny McLaughlin. He could, he reflected, have planned this better. Tramping through damp woods in the middle of the night was not his idea of fun.

Ten minutes later, while McLaughlin still lurked in the shadows of the trees, Tony was having less fun. Those miserable teenage memories flooded back with an even greater intensity as he stood by the side of the road, a hopeful thumb extended, as the traffic rushed past. Evidently he wasn't the only one who thought himself too old to be a hitch-hiker. The many disdainful looks cast in his direction by passengers in the cars flashing past him did nothing to alleviate his mood. But just as he was about to give up hope, a battered white Transit van winked its headlights at him and began to slow down. Relieved, Tony jogged towards it. A rather unprepossessing-looking youth poked his head out of the passenger window.

'Going to London?' asked Tony hopefully.

'Yeah.' Although it was dark and the youth's features were all but hidden behind a generous beard and shaggy hair, Tony reckoned he was smiling. 'Jump in if you want a lift. The more the merrier.' Tony grinned as McLaughlin approached. 'That's just as well. There are two of us.'

'No problem.' The youth nodded towards the back of the van, where the doors were being opened by as yet unseen hands.

'Hop in.'

Tony and McLaughlin looked at each other with something approaching dismay as they clambered into the vehicle. It was cluttered with musical instruments, speakers, amplifiers and what appeared to be three dead bodies.

McLaughlin raised his eyebrows as he addressed Tony. 'Nice one,' was all he said.

Tony, after an initial horrified glance at the bodies, merely grinned. They were not, he realised, dead. Just drunk. As they settled down as best they could and closed the doors behind them, the van pulled back on to the road and the man sitting beside the driver turned round and smiled through the unfashionable amount of hair. But it was his gesture rather than his appearance that worried Tony. He was holding a joint and proffering it to them. They both shook their heads, but the man was undeterred. He picked up a beer can and smiled again. 'Drink?'

Tony refused. Great, he thought, just our luck if we were picked up by the police. A van that was probably unroadworthy and a clutch of occupants who were either drunk or stoned, and probably both. He sighed as McLaughlin accepted the beer. This was going to be an eventful journey.

Had he not been so preoccupied with his new travelling companions, he might have noticed that they were being followed.

'We're a rock band,' said the driver conversationally and obviously. 'Going to do a gig at the Slug and Lettuce in Hackney. Know it?'

'Er . . . no.'

'Oh well, come along anyway. It'll be fun.'

I'm sure, thought Tony. A real riot.

'We're The Runs,' continued the driver.

'The *what*?'

'The Runs. We started life as The Trotskyists but that was too big for the posters. So we reformed as The Trots.' He laughed. 'Then we just sort of became The Runs. I'm Steve. This,' he indicated the man with the joint, 'is Rob. And those,' this time he took both hands off the wheel as he gesticulated in their general direction, 'are Vicki, Sid and Gordy. Although they're not, at the moment, really with us.' A contented snore from beside Tony corroborated this statement.

'I'm Tony.'

'And I'm Danny.' McLaughlin's Irish accent,

even on uttering three words, was unmistakable.

Steve was delighted. 'Danny Boy!' Tony and McLaughlin looked at each other in trepidation, fearing that Steve would start singing the well-known Irish song. But instead he asked them what they were doing wandering round in the middle of the night.

'We're on the run,' said Tony, 'from MI5.'

McLaughlin looked at his fellow runaway in horror. What on earth had got into him? Tony just grinned.

Steve, as Tony had suspected, was tickled. He punched the air and, in a truly dreadful American accent, yelled 'Way to go!' His shout woke the couple beside Tony in the cramped van. The girl looked at Tony through bleary eyes and then turned to her boyfriend. Without a word, they started kissing and fondling each other energetically. Tony rolled his eyes heavenwards. This was going to be a long journey.

It was also, he was glad to find out, going to be a broken journey. Half an hour later, Steve announced that they would stop for 'provisions' at an all-night café. Tony didn't ask what those provisions were. He was just glad to hear that he would be able to get out of the van. The necking couple, the smell of beer and more pungent aroma of dope were all conspiring to make him feel slightly sick. He was also glad for another reason. As the van pulled into the forecourt of the café, he turned to McLaughlin. 'I told Sarah I'd phone to find out where we should meet. Want to come with me?' McLaughlin hesitated and then shook his head. 'No. I'd better stay out of sight.

Don't,' he added, 'tell her where we are.'

Tony looked at him in amusement and gestured towards their travelling companions. 'Don't worry, I won't. She'd never believe me anyway.'

As the van shuddered to a halt outside the café, the band members clambered lethargically to their feet and made their unsteady descent from the vehicle. Tony followed suit, closing the doors behind him and hiding McLaughlin from any prying eyes.

As Tony walked across the forecourt to the telephone box in the corner, the car that had been following them pulled up behind the van. Even before it had stopped, the passenger door opened and a man hurried out. Neither Tony in the phone box nor the band members in the café could see him as he walked briskly towards the Transit van.

Tony dialled Sarah's number and waited impatiently as it kept ringing. He looked at his watch. It was past midnight. She was probably in bed.

'Hello?' said a sleepy voice just as he was about to hang up.

'Sarah? It's Tony. Sorry to get you up, but I'm just ringing to say that I've got him and that we're on the road.' As he spoke he looked idly at a car pulling out of the forecourt and accelerating swiftly away.

'Great. Everything OK?'

Tony grinned. 'Fine. We're in good company. I just wanted to establish where you want us to meet when—'

But the sentence remained unfinished. Behind Tony, the Transit van, the safe refuge of Danny McLaughlin, exploded with an ear-splitting bang, and then burst fiercely into flames. A millisecond later, the walls of the telephone box shattered, sending Tony to the ground as shards of glass splintered into his face and his hands. And as the receiver dangled from its rest, the anxious voice of Sarah Teale, almost drowned out by the roar of the flames, was shouting Tony's name. But Tony was hardly aware of it. Stunned and shaken, he sat slumped amid the splinters of glass and stared behind him at the scene of destruction. The Transit van was engulfed in flames and Danny McLaughlin was no more.

8

The camera caught Jeremy Taylor's best profile as he listened to Sarah Teale's question.

'Has the British Government,' she asked, 'ever authorised a clandestine shoot-to-kill policy?'

Jeremy looked patronisingly at her and crossed his elegant legs. 'Shoot-to-kill,' he said, 'is a media fallacy. It has never happened. It won't happen.' He leaned forward in the unconvincing gesture of sincerity so beloved by politicians. 'It will *never* happen. It's a complete myth. In the case of the Brighton shootings, the actions of the SAS were perfectly justified. You see,' he explained as if talking to a child, 'here were terrorists – armed terrorists – staging a rerun of the bombing of the Grand Hotel in 1984. No one could stand that again; the prospect of more bodies – elected representatives of the British people – being murdered and mutilated. Oh no.' He shook his head. 'Anarchy, chaos, a state of emergency. With that in mind, the actions of the SAS were wholly appropriate and fully in accordance with the law.'

'What if I told you,' answered Sarah almost as smugly, 'that there was a witness who stated that the entire operation was set up by the security services for propaganda purposes?'

The camera moved back to Jeremy Taylor and caught him looking momentarily shocked. Then he quickly recovered his composure.

'I very much doubt,' he said with total conviction, 'that you could find such a witness.'

At that point the interview disappeared from the screen as Sarah stabbed angrily at the control switch. She looked at the people sitting round her; at Harry, Tony and Mo. 'And that,' she said with a flourish, 'is what we're left with.' All four of them were now downcast and silent. The programme should have been terrific. Jeremy Taylor's self-satisfied smirk should have disappeared from the screen to be replaced by Danny McLaughlin declaring that shoot-to-kill did indeed exist, that he himself had been the MI5 informer instructed to engineer the whole incident, and that the whole point of the exercise had been to boost the Government's flagging popularity and to justify both MI5's existence and its secrecy. He would have added that, while the nation at large would neither know nor care, part of the idea was to make Special Branch look stupid. He would then have declared that the three dead men were neither armed nor terrorists and that he himself had been duped by MI5.

But instead he had been killed by MI5. They all knew it, but would never be able to prove it. Back to square one. The police had confirmed that the Transit van had been blown up by an incendiary device, and they had spent many hours interrogating the unfortunately named and shell-shocked rock band. Steve, the driver of the van, had told them they were wasting their time and would be better off questioning the surviving hitch-hiker who, he knew, had been on the run from MI5. The police had laughed.

The surviving hitch-hiker's face, criss-crossed with the scars left from the splintering glass, could have told the police some very interesting things. As he sat with the others in the editing suite, he pondered on whether to tell them what he had discovered since the 'accident' that the tabloid newspapers had so ghoulishly reported.

The day after the death of Danny McLaughlin, Tony had phoned John Deakin. Loath as he was to have anything to do with the man, Tony suspected that he knew a great deal more about the entire Brighton incident than he had admitted, and he had been right.

They had met at John Deakin's favourite meeting-place – the South Bank complex with the panoramic vista that included the headquarters of both MI5 and MI6.

'Did McLaughlin tell you much?' had been Deakin's opening gambit.

Tony had just looked at him and remained mute.

'I did hear a rumour,' continued Deakin, 'that Five were more involved in the Brighton shootings than mere intelligence-gathering would warrant.' He cast Tony a knowing look. 'McLaughlin was probably a liability even before you went crashing in.'

Tony turned in horror to Deakin. 'But you could only have known that from Branch!'

It was Deakin's turn to be non-committal.

Tony bent his head for a moment as he silently contemplated the implications of this. Then he glared angrily at Deakin. 'Branch hired you to leak information to Sarah Teale, didn't they?'

Deakin smiled.

'And so you recommended a newly available ex-police officer who happens to be a woman, right? Mo,' he continued, 'is going to just whoop with joy when she knows you were behind it all.'

Deakin smiled innocently. 'And there was me thinking you wanted to work with Maureen again.' Then, lowering his voice, he added, 'I'd keep it quiet if I were you.'

Tony looked at his companion with barely concealed disgust. 'How did Five find out I was on to McLaughlin?'

'I told them. I apologise.'

'You bastard.'

Deakin again assumed his expression of unconvincing innocence. 'I didn't know McLaughlin was Five's property. Of course, if you hadn't blundered in like a bull in a china shop, he'd still be alive.'

'He'd still be alive if you hadn't told them!' Tony shouted. 'I mean, what is this? They're going round planting bombs now?'

'MI5?' said Deakin, feigning surprise. 'Why on earth should they? The IRA wanted him too, you know.'

Tony was by now too furious to trust himself to speak. He just stared contemptuously at Deakin as the full truth dawned on him. Deakin himself smiled smugly for a moment, then walked away.

No, thought Tony as he dragged his thoughts

back to the present and his subdued companions in the editing suite of Encounter Productions. It's not worth explaining this one; it's not worth explaining that all of them had been pawns in yet another game of sickening warfare between the security services and that they had been deliberately used to fish out Danny McLaughlin and lead him to his death.

It was Sarah who broke the silence. Wanting to forget the whole thing, to dismiss from her mind a programme that should have been dynamite but had instead fizzled out with a whimper, she abruptly got to her feet and looked resignedly at her companions. 'Thanks,' she said, 'for all your help.' As the others got to their feet, she went up first to Harry and shook his hand. Then she did the same with Tony. Tony fancied her hand lingered in his for longer than it had in Harry's as she warmly bid him goodbye. Maybe, he thought, something good will come out of this after all. He was, therefore, not best pleased when Sarah went up to Mo and kissed her on the cheek. 'Thanks, Maureen – and I'm sorry. Let's meet for a drink some time.'

'Good idea,' replied Mo with a smile.

'Well,' said Harry as they walked down the street, 'quite frankly, I could do with a drink.'

'Mo's buying,' said Tony, prodding her in the ribs.

She shook her head. 'Not this time, I'm afraid. I just want to get home.'

'Is Kate all right now?' asked Tony.

Mo turned to him and gave him an odd look.

'How d'you mean?'

'Oh . . . nothing.'

'No, come on,' pressed Maureen. 'What?'

Tony looked awkward. 'Well, she just seemed a little stressed out the other night. Just a bit,' he added, trying to back-track.

'Which night?'

'The . . . er, the night you and Sarah went to Brighton.'

Mo stopped and looked threateningly at him. 'Is that supposed to mean something?'

'No.' Tony failed in his attempt to look the picture of wounded innocence. But Mo was by now distinctly annoyed. 'You think I slept with Sarah in Brighton, don't you?'

'Well, me and Harry just thought . . .' Tony looked to Harry for support.

Harry looked back in annoyance. It was news to him that he had been party to this 'just thinking'. 'Hey! Leave me out of this, Guv, do us a favour.'

Mo rounded angrily on Tony. 'I know you find it hard to imagine that a relationship can be both faithful and sexually fulfilling, but I wouldn't have thought you found it hard to recognise people's sexual orientation. Sarah,' she said with emphasis, 'didn't even spent the night in Brighton. And for your information, she isn't gay. In fact, for some reason that I find totally incomprehensible, she seems to have taken rather a shine to you.' With one last, livid look at Tony, she stomped off down the street.

Tony, looking both suitably chastised and slightly stunned, just stared at her retreating back. Beside him, Harry started to laugh. The sound

109

drew Tony away from his own thoughts. He turned and grinned broadly at his friend. Harry, he realised, hadn't laughed like that for months. Perhaps, he thought, life is beginning to get back to normal.

9

Four days later, Harry, with a spring in his step, walked into the sitting-room of Tony's flat, a room which doubled as the headquarters of Tony Clark Associates. Then he stopped in his tracks. 'What the hell . . .!' he exclaimed as he looked around him.

Tony looked up in annoyance from the piece of paper he was fiddling with. 'What d'you mean, "what the hell"?'

Harry gestured at the pieces of office machinery that hadn't been there two days previously. 'I mean, what the hell's all this?'

Tony looked proudly at his new acquisitions. 'That,' he said, 'is a computer. This is a fax. That's a new phone and answering—'

'All right!' Harry held up his hand. 'I'm not daft. I know what they are. What I want to know is why.'

'Because,' said Tony, 'we've got a new job.'

'Oh?'

'Yeah. A good one.'

'It had better be,' said Harry drily, mentally calculating the price of the new hardware.

It was. The day before, Tony had got a phone

call from the Foreign Office. Would Tony Clark, the caller had asked, care to come over to discuss a security matter that might be 'of interest' to him? Tony hadn't demurred. Any job was of interest to him and a call from the Foreign Office was extremely encouraging – it meant both money and kudos. It also meant that the job, whatever it was, would be 'above board'. No MI5, no MI6, no Special Branch – and no John Deakin. After the shoot-to-kill fiasco, Tony had had his fill of the mysterious ways of the secret security services.

The man from the Foreign Office had been young, smooth, and quietly efficient. Tony hated him on sight – he reminded him of David Graves. Yet Tony kept his opinions to himself: hating David Graves hadn't done him very much good. Henry Goode, however, merely smiled blandly at Tony and asked him a few questions about his business. Tony gave him a brief resumé of his activities since leaving the force, deliberately missing out the abortive attempts to bring Danny McLaughlin out of hiding. He wasn't proud of that particular episode.

Henry Goode, who probably knew more about what Tony had been up to than Tony himself did, was most interested in the first job he had done, in hotel security. He smiled over the table and clasped his hands in front of him. 'That,' he said, 'is why I thought you'd be suitable for this job.' He smiled again. 'It's hotel security . . . of a sort. Although it's a little more high-profile than your last assignment.'

Tony raised an eyebrow. He hadn't actually told Henry Goode many details about the last hotel job.

And why, he thought, do junior ministers from the Foreign Office always have to be so bloody patronising? Then he thought about the money he would charge for a high-profile job and, for the first time, smiled across the table in genuine pleasure. 'So what,' he asked, '*is* the job?'

Henry got to his feet. 'I can't tell you much more until I know you're going to accept. Suffice to say that you would be looking after a visiting – er – dignitary for a week. And he may need a lot of looking after.' He looked pointedly at Tony. As Danny McLaughlin hadn't officially existed, Henry was unable to mention him. But the look was enough to tell Tony that Henry knew just how well Danny had been looked after by Tony Clark Associates. No doubt Henry had been fed – and had swallowed – the line about the Transit van being blown up by the IRA. Still, what did Henry care about an Irishman who had been a positive liability when he had been alive?

Tony also stood up. 'OK, I accept,' he said.

'Good.' Henry looked at his watch. 'Now, if you'll follow me, they're expecting us at the Chilean Embassy.'

At the embassy, they had been ushered into a small room where a voluptuous, very Latin-looking woman in her forties awaited them. She rose to her feet, revealing an elegant pair of legs beneath a very short skirt and, when she smiled, a row of perfect, sparkling teeth. Tony's smile came much more easily than it had when he had been introduced to Henry Goode.

The woman extended a beautifully manicured

and heavily be-ringed hand. 'Soledad Sanchez,' she said.

'Tony Clark.'

Then the woman smiled at Henry. 'Hello, Henry. Good to see you again. I'm glad you recruited Mr Clark. I've heard good reports about him.' Her cut-glass accent matched her demeanour. Small world, he thought. A small and dangerous world.

Soledad indicated for them to sit down. 'I take it,' she said to Tony, 'that you don't know much about this project?'

'Nothing.' Then Tony smiled, remembering where he was. 'Apart from the fact that it involves Chile.'

Soledad looked from one man to the other. 'Not Chile; a Chilean. A rather high-powered one, actually. And we want you to look after him for a week. His name is General Herrera.'

'Who the fuck,' said Harry as Tony finished, 'is General Herrera?'

'Dunno.'

'You don't *know*?'

Tony stood up. Then he took the piece of paper on which he had been writing and approached the as yet unused fax machine. 'No. Apart from the fact that I correctly made the amazing deduction that he's a Chilean general, I know nothing about him. They wouldn't tell me.'

Harry looked disdainfully at Tony and his abortive attempts to send the fax. 'You telling me you bought all this fancy stuff on the strength of a week's contract working for some dodgy poxy dago?'

114

'The spook,' said Tony, 'at the FO said they'll give us bigger contracts when we've proved ourselves. And,' he added as he looked in bewilderment at the unresponsive fax machine, 'you can't turn up at Le Mans in a Robin Reliant.'

'I'm not sure if I want to work for that lot.'

'Look, Harry. They want us both round this afternoon to show us where Herrera'll be staying and then we can start asking questions. And anyway, if we put in the graft now and build up a track record, in a year's time we'll be able to pick and choose who we work for. We'll be independent.' He turned and looked meaningfully at Harry. 'Like Deakin. We won't have to answer to anybody.'

Harry didn't reply at first. Then he walked over to the fax and pressed the 'send' button. The machine whirred into life. 'It's a good idea,' he said caustically, 'to learn to walk before you try to run.'

The first fax transmission from Tony Clark Associates reached its destination just as Harry finished speaking. It arrived at the reception desk of Encounter Productions and was addressed to Sarah Teale. 'Any chance,' it read, 'of lunch this year?'

10

Henry Goode and Soledad Sanchez took Tony and Harry to the hotel that had been booked for General Herrera's visit. It was one of London's smartest and most exclusive. Foreign royalty stayed there; so did pop stars, tycoons, tyrants and anyone else who could afford the exorbitant room rates. As they walked through the opulent foyer towards the sweeping staircase, Tony looked around him and decided that the place was most unsuitable for a general from a country where violence and oppression bubbled constantly below the surface. One thing he did know about Chile was that the country's previous military regime had made a great deal of enemies and expelled huge amounts of dissidents, some of whom were resident in London. And any of them, Tony reckoned, could swan into this West End bastion of luxury and ensure that General Herrera's visit to London would be his last. It was a chance he had no intention of taking.

'He can't stay here,' he said even before he entered the suite earmarked for the General and his wife.

Soledad looked at him in surprise. 'But it's got cameras monitoring every floor and every entrance!'

'Look. I've worked in hotel security and I can tell you that those cameras are only as good as the blokes watching them.'

'The General's wife specifically asked to stay here,' replied Soledad importantly. 'I have no intention of cancelling the rooms.'

'The only back exit is through the kitchens, and the road outside could easily be blocked,' chipped in Harry. 'And there are too many people around,' he added decisively, 'to take him out the front.'

Soledad glared at him. 'There weren't any problems when General Pinochet stayed here.'

'And what were Pinochet's security arrangements?' asked Tony.

'I can't tell you that.'

'You're not telling us very much, are you? We don't even know who Herrera is, we don't know what he's doing in London, and we don't know why, if this is a private visit, as you said, he needs such tight security.' He shrugged. 'You're going to have to trust us eventually. The more we know, the better we can do the job.'

Soledad looked at him in contemplative silence and then, apparently coming to some sort of decision, she sighed. 'How much do you know about Chile, Mr Clark?'

Tony grinned. 'Well, they tend to lack discipline – especially in the penalty area.'

Harry, and even the quietly attentive Henry, laughed at that one. Soledad was not so amused. After a quick glance at Henry, she turned back to

117

Tony. 'I think we had better go back to the embassy. I think it's time I told you a bit about my country – and about General Herrera.'

Two hours later, Tony felt he'd been through a crash course in Chilean history, and he wasn't sure that he'd passed. He realised, as countless Europeans had realised before him, that his ignorance of the country was monumental. Soledad, knowing this, had sat him and Harry down the minute they returned to the embassy and proceeded to give them a potted, yet highly passionate, history of her homeland.

She told them that, for sixteen years until March 1990, Chile had been ruled by a military dictatorship under General Augusto Pinochet, and that, under his rule, the country's economy had prospered. At the mention of Pinochet, Tony raised an eyebrow. 'I seem to recall,' he said mildly, 'that Pinochet's reputation over here is not much better than Hitler's.'

Soledad sighed. 'It is difficult,' she replied wearily, 'for foreigners to understand both what Pinochet did and didn't do for our country. In 1973 he ousted President Allende in a coup which was welcomed by much of the country.' She leaned forward. 'You must understand that South America as a whole has always been a fairly . . . conservative place. Allende's Government was the first democratically elected Marxist Government in the whole continent. It made a lot of people uneasy, including,' here she looked pointedly from Tony to Harry, 'Britain and the United States.'

'So, according to you we welcomed Pinochet.'

118

Harry both looked and sounded sceptical. 'Perhaps our media got it wrong.'

'Perhaps it did.' Soledad gave him an odd look. 'But we shall come to that later. The point is,' she continued, 'Pinochet made a lot of enemies at home. You might be able to understand that.' She smiled. 'He was a firm believer in free-market economics and what has been called the trickle-down effect – the theory that wealth created by the private sector will gradually and naturally flow down to benefit the workers.'

'Sounds like a lot of bollocks to me.' Tony was scathing. 'Sounds exactly like Thatcher. And look what happened there.'

Soledad smiled uneasily. She, as a Chilean civil servant, was supposed to be apolitical, a stance not easily achieved in that country. She was also too young to remember much about the Allende years, the only time when any left-wing elements in Chile had any voice. And she wasn't sure about Tony Clark's politics. He sounded as if he hadn't approved of Margaret Thatcher. 'The point is,' she continued, 'that although Chile is once again run by an elected Government, the military is still very powerful, and General Herrera is a very powerful military man. He is, in fact, Pinochet's deputy.'

'And what's Pinochet up to nowadays?' asked Harry through a haze of cigarette smoke.

'He is still the Army commander.'

'So here we have,' said Tony as he leaned over the desk towards Soledad, 'one of the most powerful men in Chile coming to visit, a man who has made a lot of enemies, and you have chosen *us* to arrange his security. That seems a little strange to me.'

'Does it?'

Henry Goode, who had thus far sat quietly and almost unnoticed in the corner, coughed gently. 'We want,' he then said, 'to keep this visit – er – low-profile. It's not an official visit.'

'So what is it, then?'

Henry looked at Soledad. She nodded back at him. 'The Chilean Army,' he continued, 'are involved in a joint venture with Royal Ordnance to develop certain . . . military equipment. General Herrera is overseeing the Chilean end of the project.'

'In that case,' said Harry, 'why aren't Special Branch or the Diplomatic Protection Squad handling security?'

'Because, as we said, it's not an official visit.'

'But—'

'General Herrera,' interrupted Soledad, 'will be visiting the country as a private citizen. The British Government won't be involved in any way – not officially, at least.'

Tony looked genuinely perplexed. He looked from Soledad to Henry and back. 'Forgive me if I'm being dense, but am I missing something?'

Again Soledad and Henry exchanged glances. 'Not to put too fine a point on things,' said the Foreign Office junior minister, 'the Chilean military regime got their hands pretty mucky in the seventies and eighties on the – er – the human rights front—'

'In order,' interrupted Tony sarcastically, 'to benefit the economy, no doubt.'

Henry ignored the interruption. 'But on the other hand, the Chileans were very helpful during the Falklands War. Very helpful. And now there are some very lucrative military contracts in the balance.'

'I see.' Tony's words belied his expression.

Henry edged his chair closer. 'Come on, Tony, we've already indicated that there'll be some pretty lucrative contracts for you as well if you handle this one successfully. Anyway, we're only asking you to watch his back for a week.' He smiled and looked encouragingly at Tony. 'What do you say?'

Tony looked evenly back at the smooth civil servant. 'I say we ought to renegotiate our fee.'

Henry looked stony. 'I might be open to discussing that one. But not while we are here.'

'Fine.' Tony stood up and looked at Soledad. 'But I also say that there's no way, *no way* we're going to let Herrera stay at that hotel. It's a safe house or nothing.'

Soledad shrugged. 'All right. I suppose I have to agree on that one.' She picked up a pen and made a few notes on the pad in front of her. Then she smiled pleasantly at Tony. 'General Herrera will probably take it in his stride. But his wife,' she added with the suggestion of a smirk, 'will be livid.'

11

Sarah Teale always responded promptly to her mail, and it was with alacrity – and not a little delight – that she responded to the fax from Tony. Since the McLaughlin business she had thought about him often, and both those thoughts and their very existence surprised her. He wasn't, she kept telling herself, 'her sort'. So why on earth did she keep thinking about him? Perhaps it was the way he approached his work: he seemed almost completely impervious to danger, yet he always gave the impression of being in control. As she looked at the fax she had been holding for far too long, she decided that she *would* agree to have lunch – if only, she told herself, to find out why the supposedly impoverished Tony Clark and his Associates had got themselves a smart-looking new letterhead and a fax machine. Maybe he had a lucrative new contract. She grinned. Maybe he would pay for lunch this time.

They met in the same restaurant as before. And no, Tony had laughed over the phone, he wouldn't do a runner again. He would arrive with a credit card and even, he added proudly, his own mobile phone. So, mused Sarah as she put the phone down, things *were* looking up for him.

Tony, his scars from the explosion now almost completely healed, looked casual, relaxed and happy. Sarah looked exceedingly smart in a short black skirt and cream linen jacket. She also looked, and indeed appeared to be, rather downcast.

'Not trouble at home, I trust?' asked Tony nosily as he poured her a glass of wine. Sarah hadn't told him where she lived or, more importantly, if she lived with anyone else. She didn't look the sort that would stand for a live-in parent; it was highly unlikely that she had a flat-mate, but it didn't seem improbable that she might be one of those maddening media types who appeared to be entirely independent, who flirted with ease, and yet who had been living with a long-term lover for years. He had fallen for one of those in the past. All he knew about Sarah's home life was that it was conducted in the Butler's Wharf area – and he only knew that because he had looked up her home number in the area-code phone book. Sarah grinned at his question. She knew, by now, quite a lot about Tony. Since the abortive shoot-to-kill programme, she had met up with Mo for the drink she had promised and the conversation had drifted, not without a little prompting from Sarah, to the subject of Tony. She now knew about his ex-wife Sue, about the policewoman girlfriend who had committed suicide, about the totally unsuitable (according to Mo) married woman

123

from a hush-hush department and about the current void in his love-life. She also knew that he was 'nosey as hell'. When Mo had told her that, Sarah had retorted – rather prissily, she now realised – that nosiness was probably bred from years of being obliged to ask people questions. 'Crap,' had been Mo's succinct answer. Then she had laughed and told Sarah that even if he did pry too often he was one hell of a friend. Not many bosses in the overwhelmingly macho and chauvinistic environment of the Met would have been so supporting to a lesbian colleague. And, she had added, Tony had been touchingly good with Harry when he had been in danger of going off the rails after his wife's death. He might be a bastard at times, Mo had finished, but at least he was a nice one.

Sarah looked into Tony's penetrating blue eyes and decided that she liked nice bastards. Then she took a contemplative sip of wine and told him that no, things on the home front were just dandy.

'Well, that's nice,' said Tony grudgingly, 'so why are you looking so grumpy?'

'I'm not looking grumpy!'

'Yes you are.'

'No I'm not!' Then she laughed. 'This conversation is about to become distinctly childish.'

Tony grinned wickedly. 'No it's not.'

'Yes it is, and before it degenerates completely I'll admit that I *was* feeling a bit glum when I came in, but I'm all right now.'

'Good. I'm glad I have that effect on you.'

Sarah pretended she hadn't heard him. 'Wine, of course, has an enormously restorative effect, don't you think?'

'Touché,' replied Tony as he sipped the Chardonnay. It was, he had to admit, a cool little number. And not the only one around here. 'So why,' he continued, 'were you feeling so glum?'

'Oh, business. I thought a proposal of mine was going to be commissioned by the BBC, but then they changed the editor of the series and the new guy doesn't like it.' She sighed and then shrugged. 'Win some, lose some – that's the name of the game.' She looked at him again. 'It's not as if I haven't been there before.'

'No, I'm sure.'

Then the waiter marched over and, as waiters do, ordered them to give their orders. They did.

'So what about you?' asked Sarah as the waiter sauntered off. 'What are you up to?'

Tony shrugged. 'Oh, nothing much.'

'So why the new fax machine and fancy letterhead?'

'Wow!' said Tony. 'You don't miss a trick, do you?'

'I'm a journalist, remember.'

'I'll make sure I never forget.'

'So?' persisted Sarah.

'Well, it's not much, but me 'n' Harry have got a contract from . . . from a client who might put more things our way if we get this one right.'

'And what is it you have to get right?'

Tony laughed. 'You don't give up, do you? All

we're doing is looking after a visiting businessman for a week. It's nothing much.'

Sarah diverted her attention to the olives which the waiter had deposited in the middle of the table along with a basket of bread. 'No, doesn't sound too exciting. Still, as you say, if it leads to other things . . . Where,' she asked almost disinterestedly as she dipped some bread into the olive oil, 'is this chap from?'

Tony thought for a moment before replying. Her incessant questions were probably prompted by nothing more than habit. Anyway, what harm could it do mentioning the name of a country? 'Chile,' he said.

Sarah's pulse quickened almost instantaneously. Chile, she thought, this is too good to be true. Then she disguised her immediate interest by adopting a wistful expression. 'I was there a couple of years ago. It's incredibly beautiful and unspoilt, but only because all the political trouble kept the tourists out.'

'They had a coup, didn't they?'

'Mmm. In '73. Pinochet set about killing just about anyone he considered a subversive. The usual story.'

'But he's not running things now.'

'No. He called for an election assuming he'd win, but the democrats walked it and formed a Government. The military are still very powerful, though. They're a sort of parallel Government. Apparently Pinochet rolls the tanks past the presidential palace once in a while just to let everyone know he's still around.'

'So who's in the presidential palace?'

'Eduardo Frei. He was originally president before Allende – the one who promised social reform and scared the pants off the United States. Luckily for the Americans,' she added drily, 'the military coup happened and Pinochet took over. There was nothing left-wing about him, I can assure you.' Tony was looking both interested and slightly wary. 'You seem to know a lot about the place.'

Sarah took a deep breath. 'Well,' she said airily, 'it's an interesting subject.'

'Fascinating.'

'It is. It is.' She leaned back as the waiter approached with their plates and asked, in what she hoped was a casual way, what Tony's businessman did in Chile.

Tony grinned at her. This was going too far. He had, after all, just sworn never to forget that she was a journalist. 'I didn't ask.'

It *must* be, thought Sarah. It must be General Herrera. The 'little bird' she had mentioned to Mo as they were driving down to Brighton had subsequently informed her that the Chilean in charge of negotiating the arms deal with the British Government was none other than Pinochet's deputy, General Herrera. And if Tony was going to be in charge of Herrera's security, it was too good an opportunity to waste. A programme would have to be made, and Sarah's preliminary researches had already told her that such a programme could be dynamite.

Sarah had been mulling over the idea of a Chilean programme for weeks, and now, with General Herrera's visit, she had a peg to hang it on. The only problem, of course, was Tony. If he had any idea of what she was planning he would be livid, and justifiably so. She was planning to use him to gain access to Herrera. For a brief moment, she felt a twinge of regret: she was genuinely attracted to Tony, and this latest development would not exactly contribute to the development of their relationship. Then she shrugged. Too bad, she thought. Work, yet again, would have to come first.

In the past few weeks, Sarah had found out quite a lot about Chile, and none of it was particularly pleasant. The best that could be said for the Pinochet regime, as Soledad had told Harry and Tony, was that it had given the country a fairly stable economy, if not by European standards then at least by South American ones. The worst that could be said hadn't, as far as Sarah was concerned, yet been voiced. The sixteen years of military dictatorship had been, for many Chileans, a reign of terror. In the coup of 1973 that had brought Pinochet to power, over a thousand people had been killed. In the following years, countless thousands had died, and many more thousands had disappeared. No one she had talked to was able to estimate accurately how many had been tortured, but she had found out that one million Chileans were currently living in exile. Not bad, she thought, for a population of 14 million.

But what really interested Sarah, from the point

of view of her proposed documentary, was Chile's relationship with Britain throughout the Pinochet years. Publicly, the few politicians ever interviewed about Chile had decried the brutal regime. They had all cited the appalling record of the country on the human rights front, and had then tried to score points for their own Government by claiming that Britain was emphatically *not* supporting Pinochet.

It depended, thought Sarah wryly, on what you meant by support. She reckoned that active participation in their thriving arms industry counted as pretty firm support. She also reckoned that Britain's reliance on Chile during the Falklands War counted as support. The British public, she thought angrily, was and still is unaware that Britain couldn't have won that war without Chile. Ports like Punto Arenas in the south of the country had – so she had been informed by a Falklands vet – resembled Plymouth during the war: they had been chock-a-block with British war and supply ships. No newspapers had been allowed to report that, and, when the press had got wind of the fact that an SAS helicopter had crashed in southern Chile, the Government's response had been that 'nobody knew what it was doing there'. It had, of course, been based there. And for those British people who still believed that the Falklands War had been a waste of lives and nothing more than a propaganda exercise for the Thatcher Government, Sarah thought she had the answer: they were absolutely right. If Argentina had been spoiling for a fight with anybody, it was with neighbouring Chile, not with distant Britain. No wonder

Chile had lent every possible support to Britain's cause: their expensive and dirty work was being done for them.

Sarah's problem, as far as her programme was concerned, was how to link an historical war with a contemporary visit by a Chilean general. She would need, she reckoned, more up-to-date information about the British-Chilean arms connection. She got it in the shape of the arms-to-Iraq controversy. Britain, she discovered to her horror, had laundered arms for Iraq through Chile, thereby supporting two brutal regimes, and helping to precipitate another war. Britain, she felt, had a lot to answer for. And she was not the first person to think that: in 1992, an investigative freelance journalist from London had gone to Chile to try to uncover the arms-to-Iraq connection. He failed. He was found dead, hanging from the wardrobe in a room in one of the best hotels in Santiago. Oddly – and ominously – his death had gone largely unreported, and the reasons for his visit to Chile had not been given. But Sarah knew all the reasons: she had got them from his still-grieving and extremely bitter girlfriend.

Sarah had no doubt, then, that her programme had the potential to cause enormous embarrassment to, and demand explanations from, the British Government. But it would help her immeasurably if she could gain access to General Herrera and find out more about the negotiations that were the reason for his 'unofficial' visit to Britain. Tony, of course, would be furious, but that was just too bad.

So excited was Sarah, so single-minded was she about her idea, that it failed to occur to her that the other people who had trodden this same route were no longer alive.

12

General Santiago Herrera and his wife arrived at
Heathrow in a private jet. By 9 a.m., Tony and
Harry had parked their two hired Range Rovers
outside the VIP Centre and were waiting with
Soledad Sanchez inside the building. Tony, wearing a smart blue suit and a rather more sombre tie
than was his custom, was outwardly calm but
inwardly nervous. Harry, who somehow managed
to look scruffy despite his newly pressed suit, was
chainsmoking, a sign of nervousness in most
people but of normality in Harry. Soledad was
looking spectacular in a chic black suit with gold
buttons and her raven hair was tied back in a
chignon. Tony kept giving her sidelong glances.
She was, he had to admit, an exceedingly attractive
woman – but so was Sarah Teale, and at the
moment his thoughts were too full of the producer
to accommodate anything more than a fleeting
interest in anyone else. For a brief moment he
thought back to his lunch with Sarah. Now that
they weren't working together, they had, he
reckoned, developed an easy camaraderie. And he
hoped they would never work together again.

Mixing business with pleasure was fatal: the appallingly hurtful ending of his relationship with Angela Barrett was a still poignant reminder of the truth of that maxim.

Tony's thoughts were dragged back to the matter in hand by the stately procession of six individuals from the plane to the VIP Centre. He straightened his tie as Soledad came up to him and whispered, 'That's Herrera in the middle, and that,' she added with a hint of disparagement, 'is his wife Doña Hilda.' Tony looked through the window at the oddly matched couple. Herrera, even dressed in what was obviously an expensive European suit, betrayed an unmistakably military bearing. Tall and dignified with a shock of black hair peppered with grey, he looked like a man in control; a man not to be crossed.

His wife also looked like the sort of woman used to having her own way. Yet a certain petulance about her expression suggested that, where her husband might use force, she would use feminine wiles. Like the general, she appeared to be in her fifties. Small and solid, she was wearing a vivid mauve suit and, apparently, her entire collection of jewellery. She was also wearing far too much make-up. Soledad, evidently, did not think Doña Hilda a credit to her gender. She could have told Tony that the woman was a perfect example of what is known in South America as a 'mummy' — someone who is living in a previous age.

The three men surrounding them were, unmistakably, their bodyguards. Dark, thick-set and squat, they had all the tell-tale signs of rural rather than urban Chileans. They looked, by European

133

standards, extraordinarily unsophisticated, and Tony couldn't help grinning as he noted that, despite the grey and overcast morning, they all sported regulation sunglasses. But it was the fourth man who really drew Tony's attention. 'Osvaldo del Canto,' whispered Soledad. 'The General's personal bodyguard.' Del Canto looked almost as commanding as his boss. Taller and older than the other bodyguards, he alone did not sport sunglasses, and his small, black eyes spoke of extreme alertness and, thought Tony for some reason, extraordinary meanness.

The party entered the lobby of the building and Soledad stepped forward to greet the General with an effusive flood of Spanish. Then she motioned for Harry and Tony to step forward. 'This,' she said to Herrera, 'is Mr Clark, who is organising security for the visit.' Tony almost noticeably puffed up his chest as he approached the General, and there followed a little pantomime born of cultural misunderstanding.

The problem was age. Tony was younger than Harry, and General Herrera, with the customary South American reverence for age, couldn't understand why he should be in charge. For a moment he stood, a puzzled expression creasing his already wrinkled brow. Then, figuring that Soledad had made a mistake, he ignored Tony and made to shake Harry's hand. Harry, equally puzzled, returned the gesture. Tony, deflated, looked in annoyance at Soledad, who again went up to the General and politely informed of the pecking order of the British duo. Herrera was unimpressed. He had clearly already decided that he preferred the quietly professional-looking Harry to the posturing Tony, and made this clear by shaking Harry's hand before going up to Tony. 'How do you do, Mr Clark?' he said in formal, heavily accented English.

Tony smiled thinly in response. 'General Herrera.' Then he turned and indicated the highly amused Harry. 'This,' he added, 'is my *associate*, Mr Naylor.'

Again Herrera shook hands with Harry. 'I am pleased to meet you, Mr Naylor.'

Soledad broke the embarrassed silence by gesturing for the taller of the bodyguards to come forward. 'This,' she said to Tony, 'is General Herrera's head of security, Mr del Canto.' Tony and del Canto shook hands and eyed each other warily, which silently suggested an immediate rivalry between them. Neither liked the look of the other.

Doña Hilda, meanwhile, displayed not a flicker of interest in the men responsible for her security – she was far too busy overseeing a collection of the vast amount of luggage accompanying her and her husband. Bossily instructing porters to dispatch the various suitcases to the waiting Range Rovers, she missed the exchanges between the Chilean and the English contingents. Once outside, she happily climbed into the back of the first vehicle and watched as Harry and the Chilean guards loaded luggage into the boot. She also watched, without much interest, as Soledad picked up the holdall that she had taken with her to the airport and handed it to Osvaldo del Canto. The Chilean smiled in satisfaction as he took it, jumped into the passenger seat, and placed it securely in his lap.

Tony, keen that they should be on their way as soon as possible, ushered Herrera and Soledad into the seat beside Doña Hilda and then, checking that Harry and the other guards were ready to go in the other vehicle, he jumped into the driver's seat, started the engine and pulled away. He noticed del Canto opening the holdall and couldn't stop himself from trying to see the contents. Whatever they were, they seemed to make del Canto very happy.

But the job of driving away from the airport both quickly and sedately needed all his attention. This, he had known from the beginning, was one of the potential danger-spots of Herrera's schedule: it would not have been difficult for anyone with a grudge against the Chilean General to find out when and where his plane would be landing. And, he constantly reminded himself, there were a lot of people with a grudge against Herrera. Most of the one million Chileans resident outside their native country had not left by choice. They had been expelled, many of their relations had been killed and, notwithstanding that Herrera was seen by some as a 'moderate', many held him jointly responsible with Pinochet for their misfortunes.

Suddenly, just as he was about to change into fourth gear, Tony was forced to stamp on the brakes. A man, shouting obscenities in a foreign language, leaped out in front of the car and planted himself securely in the middle of the road. Harry, close behind Tony, nearly collided with him as he too slammed on his brakes. And then, in a matter of seconds, the two vehicles were surrounded by a swarm of people, all shouting abuse and some of them waving banners. It was clear that, just as Tony had feared, Herrera's arrival had been anticipated by people other than himself.

Tony ran a sticky hand over his forehead. 'Oh, Jesus, where the hell did they come from?'

Beside him, with a set expression on his face, Osvaldo del Canto rummaged in the holdall and, unseen by Tony, produced an automatic handgun. Tony began to edge the car forward through the throng of protesters, but at the all-too-familiar sound of a weapon being cocked he whirled round to face del Canto. 'For Christ's sake!' Leaning forward to try to stop the Chilean, he was again diverted – this time by the unfamiliar, unexpected and wholly unwelcome sensation of the windscreen being obliterated before his eyes. His vision was completely blocked by a great sea of red as one of the protesters hurled a bucket of paint at the vehicle. 'Shit, shit, *shit*!' Tony pulled frantically at the windscreen washer and sighed in relief as both water and the action of the wipers began to remove the paint. Pandemonium reigned both inside and outside the car. Beside Tony, del Canto was swearing loudly in Spanish and trying desperately to open his window to brandish his weapon at the angry crowd. Behind him, Doña Hilda was in hysterics, Soledad was trying to soothe her, and only General Herrera remained calm and unruffled. Evidently, this was nothing compared to some of the demonstrations he had survived in his home country.

The hurling of the paint was, in fact, a blessing in disguise. The demonstrators instinctively moved away to avoid being covered in it, and Tony saw his

137

chance of accelerating out of trouble. With Harry hot on his heels, he sped past the shouting crowd. But he wasn't quick enough to escape the notice of eyes far more intrusive than those of the protesters. The exiles had obviously sensed that Herrera's visit to Britain would be a great PR opportunity for their own cause, and, to Tony's horror, he noticed several professional-looking video crews scrambling to get direct shots of the occupants of the cars. He swore loudly as a camera was thrust right up against the window. So much, he thought, for General Herrera's discreet arrival in Britain.

Only when they were a good half-mile from the scene of the protest did he dare allow himself a sigh of relief, but even then it was short-lived. Del Canto was sitting beside him and, although he had replaced his weapon in the holdall, he was still in possession of lethal and illegal firearms. Tony caught Soledad's eye in the mirror. 'Where,' he said as calmly as he could, 'did those guns come from?'

'They were sent ahead to the embassy. Customs weren't going to let them through with us.'

'Of course they bloody weren't! It's illegal to carry guns here. Christ almighty, we could be arrested for this!'

Osvaldo del Canto turned to him and grinned a lupine grin. 'We all,' he said complacently, 'have diplomatic status.' Tony turned furiously on him. 'That doesn't mean you can go around shooting demonstrators. For Christ's sake . . .' Then, this time catching Herrera's eye in the mirror, he trailed off. The day, he realised, had not started off too well. If he was going to make a good impression on Herrera, and consequently and more importantly on the Foreign Office, he would have to go easy on the hysterics. There would be plenty of time for those when he got del Canto on his own. For now, he would concentrate on transporting his party to the safe house without further mishap.

The safe house he had rented was one that the security services often used for lodging witnesses and informants to serious national and international crimes. It was the sort of place where, he reflected ruefully, MI5 should have sheltered the now-deceased Danny McLaughlin. But then maybe not. MI5 had had no further use for McLaughlin: they had ceased to give him protection, with catastrophic and, to them, welcome results. The sight and sound of the exploding Transit van was still vivid in Tony's mind. If it had any positive effect at all, it was to remind Tony that, in the sort of job he was now doing, vigilance was of utmost importance. As he headed the little convoy through Berkshire towards the isolated safe house, he hoped that Harry, behind him, was being equally vigilant. As far as Tony himself could tell, nobody was following them, but Harry would have a clearer view of what, if anything, was happening behind them on the motorway. As for what was happening in the back seat of Tony's own vehicle, he was unable to tell. Doña Hilda was chattering away at breakneck speed in her native language, Soledad made a few dutiful responses and Herrera, apart from the odd gruff exchange with del Canto, remained silent. Tony found his silence oppressive: it seemed to radiate disapproval in the direction of the driver's seat.

Ten minutes after pulling off the motorway, Tony thankfully turned into a minor road and, shortly afterwards, through the impressive-looking metal gates of the safe house. He breathed another sigh of relief as he pulled up outside the house. Home, he thought.

Doña Hilda, however, thought otherwise. As soon as they had turned into the drive and the house came into view, her chatter ceased and her mouth closed into a hard little line. While the gates had been promising, the house itself was anything but. It was an ordinary, slightly ugly 1930s building with little to recommend it. It wasn't, she noticed with distaste, even very big. Doña Hilda Herreras was used to better things, if only because she had married the General, a man who came from a long line of military bigwigs. Her own antecedents were somewhat more humble.

Hilda Hernandez had been born in northern Chile into a family which had long been involved in the copper industry. To her eternal regret, her father, like his father before him, had been a manager of a big copper mine, not its owner. From an early age, Hilda had been ambitious for better things, and for a woman in Chile, better things meant belonging to the hugely powerful and vastly wealthy upper classes. Unlike most other South American countries, Chile had long had a burgeoning middle class, a section of society to which the Hernandez family firmly belonged. And like middle classes everywhere, they had aspirations. Hilda's aspirations took her to higher education in

Santiago, not because she was interested in furthering her academic career, but because Santiago and the surrounding central plain of Chile was home to the tiny section of society which still believed that their bloodlines, titles and famous surnames made them God's chosen people. To Hilda's intense irritation, God appeared to be looking elsewhere when she was trying to inveigle herself into the upper classes. The chosen ones were very open to ideas and people from abroad, and especially from Europe and the United States, yet they were extraordinarily closed to anything Chilean, unless its value had been proven abroad. Thus they were closed to Hilda Hernandez, a Chilean upstart who had never left the country.

Hilda, however, was no fool. While many Chilean aristocrats purported to despise the military, they were constantly aware that their own interests were best served by keeping the military muscle both powerful and high-profile. Both factions were extremely right-wing, and both felt that the theory of democracy was acceptable as long as it did not upset the unequal social order. And while the military relished its power, it represented, from Hilda's point of view, an easier target than the aristocracy.

In 1958, Hilda met and married Santiago Herrera, then a captain in the Chilean Army. It was, as both of them were thirty, a relatively late marriage, yet it was a spectacularly successful one. Both were ambitious, and they complemented each other perfectly. As Santiago rose through the ranks, so Hilda rose socially.

The election of Eduardo Frei to the Chilean

presidency in 1964 appeared, at first, to be a setback to both Hilda and Santiago. The wife had begun to make friends with the 'Hacienda Set' – the landowning classes to which she had long aspired – and the husband had been promoted yet again. But with Frei's attempts at land reform, the huge estates and their owners came under threat, and, as Frei was the first president in Chilean history to have at least theoretical control of both the Government executive and legislature, the Army became less of a political force.

Worse was to come for the likes of the Herreras when, in 1969, Salvador Allende was elected. As socialist reformer, he was regarded by many, and especially by the United States, as a communist and a potentially lethal threat everywhere. And he was particularly despised by the *momios* or mummies – people like Hilda. By 1973, the Army had had enough, and staged a coup, seizing power and – although they never admitted to it – killing Allende. General Augusto Pinochet, previously loyal to Allende, became the dictator of the permanent Army-led Government which was to last for nearly seventeen years. For many Chileans, it was a disaster: the labour movement was banned; hundreds of thousands were either shot, imprisoned or driven into exile; a secret police force rounded up malcontents and kept an eye on dissenters within the armed forces, and the judiciary was cowed into submission. But for Doña Hilda the military coup was manna from heaven: her husband was one of Pinochet's closest friends and the head of the secret police. Doña Hilda Herrera had finally arrived.

Arriving in Britain, therefore, at what she perceived as a nasty, ugly suburban house instead of at Claridges was a huge comedown. At home, the Herreras were treated like royalty, even if the older aristocracy secretly regarded them as pushy *parvenus*. Doña Hilda, felt her first trip to Britain should resemble a regal procession.

Her face darkened even further when she entered the hallway of the safe house. Furiously, she turned on her husband. '*Por Dios, esta casa es una cueva de ratones. Porque no podemos ir al Hotel Clardiges como Lucia y Augusto?*'

Herrera looked resignedly at his wife. '*Por favor, estoy muy cansado — sólo quiero descansar.*'

Tony, standing with Harry behind the Herreras, noted this heated exchange and, frowning, approached the worried Soledad. 'Is there a problem?' he whispered. His command of Spanish was nil, but it didn't take a linguist to tell that Doña Hilda was not best pleased.

Soledad looked at him with an 'I told you so' expression. 'She wants to stay where the Pinochets stayed.'

'Over my dead body.'

As Tony spoke, the Herreras advanced into the sitting-room and, without turning round, shut the door behind them. Clearly, they felt no need to stand on ceremony where their bodyguards were concerned. Their voices, and Doña Hilda's high-pitched, petulant tones in particular, could still be heard from behind the door.

Tony sighed. 'At least we weren't followed here. Those bloody protesters.' He looked darkly at Soledad. 'What I'd like to know is how they found out when and where Herrera was arriving.'

Soledad shrugged. 'Probably from the embassy. It leaks like a sieve. And anyway, it's not the sort of information that's difficult to come by.'

'Did you recognise any of them?' asked Tony.

'They were, I think, mostly Chileans who were exiled here.'

'Hmm.' Again he looked at her. 'Is there anything else I ought to know?'

Soledad walked across the hallway to where the Chilean bodyguards had deposited the Herreras' immodest amounts of luggage. Then she turned and smiled at Tony. 'Not that I can think of at the moment.'

Tony, puzzled and slightly disconcerted by her composure in the face of their recent near-disaster, went off to find Harry. Chileans, he mused, were a funny lot.

Harry, in the security room of the safe house, was thinking the same thing. The three junior bodyguards who were with him had paid not the blindest bit of attention to his pleas that they should not wear their semi-automatic weapons. The word 'illegal' seemed to cut absolutely no ice. And his attempts to explain the security system to them met with blank stares. Patiently, he went over to the control panel and began to fiddle with the joystick in the middle of it. The stick, he explained, moved the cameras placed all over the house, which in turn fed back to the screen above the control panel. 'You can cover,' he added, 'all of the front of the house this way.'

The guard who had introduced himself as Luís

looked at Harry in amusement as he operated the joystick. '*Es como jugando al Nintendo, no?*'

The other two, Antonio and Jorge, laughed uproariously. Harry, whose command of Spanish was rivalled only by Tony's, had at least understood one word. He grinned. 'Nintendo, right.' These guys, he thought, weren't a bad lot. They seemed friendly enough, if a little laid-back. He hoped, without much conviction, that their attitude towards their firearms would be a little less relaxed.

At that moment, a disgruntled-looking Tony walked in accompanied by Osvaldo del Canto. From the expressions on both of their faces, it was evident that they had still failed to establish a friendly rapport. Tony looked fleetingly at Harry and raised his eyebrows. 'I'm just going to show him how to arm the system.'

Harry nodded as Tony went over to the panel on the far wall and put a key into the prominent keyhole flanked by several lights and arrows. As he turned the key, a red light went on. Addressing del Canto, he explained, 'You just turn it to the right to activate the whole system. None of the windows in the house open more than three inches, and they're all bulletproof.' He turned to see if del Canto was listening. The other three, still pretending they were playing Nintendo, were clearly not. But del Canto, he was relieved to notice, was riveted. 'The only way into this place is through the front door,' continued Tony, 'and through the entrance to the garage. And both of those entrances are reinforced with steel plate.' Unlike, he could have added, the doors of Claridges. Del

Canto nodded. 'Fine. That seems all right. But do you have another key?'

'No. There's only the one. That way there can't be any confusion about who has it.'

'In which case, I think I ought to take it.'

Tony bit his lip. Watch yourself, Tone, he thought. No need to antagonise the brute. He straightened his shoulders and smiled pleasantly at del Canto. 'With all due respect, I'm responsible for the security of the house. I think I'd better hang on to it.'

Del Canto raised his eyebrows and looked directly into Tony's eyes. Tony had been told on many occasions that his icy gaze was cold enough to 'freeze the balls of a brass monkey', but his penetrating blue eyes had nothing on the Chilean's hard, gimlet-like black ones. He stared back and forced a smile. Soledad, opening the door with a flourish, broke the ensuing uneasy silence. She entered the room, weighed down under a huge stack of files. Depositing them on the table, she looked at Tony. 'I forgot to tell you; I've had these sent over from the embassy. It's everything we have on all active Chilean dissidents in London and the Chilean Exile Centre.'

Tony groaned inwardly. A fist-fight with del Canto would be preferable to sifting through that lot. But as he stared at the heap of thick buff folders, an idea came to him. It was, he thought, an excellent idea.

13

Maureen was fed up. For the first time in years she had nothing to do, and idleness did not come easily to her. Having been brought up in Aberdeenshire, she had, from an early age, been instilled with the Protestant work ethic. Some of her older relations at home still trotted out phrases like 'the Devil finds work for idle hands' and, remembering this with amusement, she wondered what they would say if they could see her now. Although it was well past midday, she was still in her dressing-gown, lying on the sofa in the sitting-room, flicking indolently through the pages of *Cosmopolitan*. She hadn't yet identified anything devilish about the magazine, but she had quickly established one thing about it: it wasn't aimed at her. She was too old.

Too old. What a grim little phrase, she thought. She was also, at thirty-five, too old to be unemployed, too old to have to think about a change of career, and too old to spend half her days bickering like an adolescent with her lover. Since she had been ignominiously booted out of the force, her relationship with Kate had deteriorated. The brief stint working for Sarah Teale at Encounter Productions, although it had boosted her self-esteem, had done little for her love-life. She had been more amused than annoyed that Tony had thought she was having an affair with Sarah, but more than a little upset when she discovered that Kate had been thinking along the same lines.

She and Kate had had a terrible showdown about that. Mo had launched into Kate for being so untrusting; Kate had got at Mo for being surly and uncommunicative. Then the real cause of Kate's unease had come to light: she admitted to Mo that she was terrified about her joining forces once more with Tony and Harry. After that they had made up. Mo, quite genuinely, had told Kate that there was no way she was even considering joining Tony Clark Associates. As she had told Tony himself, the shoot-to-kill business had been a one-off. Now she was going to get a safe job; not, probably, a job as interesting as Kate's management consultancy work, but a safe, secure, pensionable job nonetheless.

There were, however, not many jobs like that for an ex-policewoman. It had been hard enough for Mo to persuade people at interviews that, no, her work at the Met and at CIB had not involved plodding the pavements directing American tourists towards Harrods but had, in fact, been demanding, dangerous and both physically and mentally challenging. There was a lot of learning, a lot of theory, a lot of research and a great deal of inter-personal skills involved in being in 'the job'. But somehow, she had failed to get that across to prospective employers. More often than not, they viewed her as a creature from another planet.

Added to that, Mo was increasingly feeling that a nine-to-five job would be anathema to her. Again, the dreaded phrase 'too old' came to mind. And *Cosmopolitan* was no help at all; the article she had just finished was entitled 'You're Never Too Old to Change', and was accompanied by a picture of a tanned, smiling 'career woman' who had to be all of seventeen. In disgust, Maureen threw the magazine to the other end of the room. It landed, slid along the highly polished wooden floor and came to rest under the other sofa. Good, she thought. Out of sight and out of mind. Then she yawned and contemplated what to do for the rest of the day. She could, she supposed, carry on tiling the bathroom, but even that was beginning to depress her. Harry had helped her with the DIY when she and Kate had first moved in, but now he had better things to do. Now he was working.

The loud ring of the doorbell jolted Maureen out of her increasingly maudlin reverie. She jumped to her feet and then looked guiltily down at her attire. She was alarmed to find herself wondering what the neighbours would think if they saw her answering the front door in a dressing-gown at lunchtime. 'Oh, *sod* the neighbours!' she shouted out loud as she went into the hall. They already had their suspicions about Kate and her anyway. Two grown women living together and rarely a man about the place. *Very* odd.

The neighours, however, would have been pleased to see who was at the door. So was Mo. It was Tony, looking extremely smart and smiling broadly.

'Hello,' he said. 'Sorry to get you up.'

Maureen poked out her tongue at him. 'You did *not* get me up. I was . . . well, I was reading.' Thank God *Cosmopolitan* had disappeared under the sofa. Then she grinned at him. 'Well, I suppose you'd better come in. We don't want to upset the neighbours.'

'Indeed we don't.' Tony sauntered into the open-plan sitting-room and looked around. 'Very tidy in here.'

'Is that a compliment or a criticism?'

'It's a compliment. I want a cup of coffee as a reward.'

'OK. Come into the kitchen and tell me what you're doing here. And tell me,' she added over her shoulder, 'what you're doing carrying those nasty-looking files.' Under his arm, Tony was carrying some of the files Soledad had given him.

'I've come,' he said as he sat down at the kitchen table, 'to offer you a job.'

'A job?' Maureen glared at him. 'What sort of job?'

Tony grinned. 'Is that the way you react to all prospective employers?'

Maureen sighed and looked away, pretending to busy herself with the coffee paraphernalia. Bugger it, she thought. *Bugger* it. Here I am, trying my best to persuade myself I want a proper job and along comes Tony to mess it all up. She turned back to him. 'You're not the sort of employer I want, Tony. You know that. I want . . . oh, I want security and . . . and . . .'

'I'm not offering you a permanent job, Mo. Just a few days' work. It'll help tide you over.' He looked her in the eye. 'It was you, after all, who told me how much you hated being financially dependent on Kate.'

Oh, go for the jugular, why don't you? thought Maureen in irritation. Then she checked herself before replying. She had, it was true, nothing to lose. 'OK, then. I'm listening – but I'm not committing myself.'

Tony smiled. Good, he thought, Mo's on board. 'What d'you know,' he said, 'about Chile?'

'Chile?'

'Yes. The country in South America. Not the pepper.'

'Ha ha.' Mo frowned. Someone, recently, had mentioned Chile to her, but she couldn't remember who, or in what context. She shrugged. 'Not a lot. Why?'

'Because I've got a contract to look after a visiting Chilean general for a week and I'd like you to help me.'

Mo snorted. 'I know enough about Chile to know that its generals aren't very nice men. They had the most brutal military dictatorship, you know.'

'So they say.' Tony was deliberately evasive. 'But not any more. They've got a democracy now.'

'Oh, bully for them. So do we, and look where that's got us.'

'Mo, I'm not here to talk politics. I'm just here to ask if you want to earn a hundred a day helping me make sure nobody gets at Herrera.'

'Herrera? He was Pinochet's deputy, wasn't he?'

Tony, impressed, looked up at Mo. 'How the hell did you know that?'

151

'I read newspapers, Tony. And sometimes I don't like what I read. Especially about people like Pinochet and Herrera. They had a reign of terror going in Chile, you know. They expelled about a million people and tortured God knows how many others.' She shook her head vehemently and then sipped the newly brewed coffee. 'Sorry, Tony, no can do. I'm not overburdened with scruples, but one thing I'm not going to do is shake hands with people like Herrera.'

'Ah, but that's just the point. You won't even have to meet him. All you'll have to do is look into these.' He patted the stack of files beside him on the table. 'They contain information on Chilean dissidents.'

'Innocent people who were forced into exile, you mean.'

Tony sighed. He'd give it one last go. 'I was hoping,' he said carefully, 'that you'd help me find out whether any of them have either the idea or the wherewithal to get at Herrera. You know, just a spot of research to see if anyone's planning to assassinate him. We were met with a riot at the airport. It was very unpleasant. And two wrongs,' he finished, 'don't make a right. Killing him wouldn't achieve anything.'

'Apart from making you look a fool.'

'Exactly.'

They looked at each other. Mo wished she hadn't made that last remark. Now, instead of a job, she'd turned his request, without any prompting, into a favour for a mate. She sat down. 'Look, I'm looking for something a bit more normal, you know? PAYE, office gossip,

152

arguments about the holiday rota. Anything that doesn't involve ballistics.'

Bullshit, thought Tony. You're not convincing yourself and you're certainly not convincing me. 'This won't involve ballistics,' he said quietly. 'You'll just get in there and find out where these . . . these dissidents are getting their information from, and what else they're planning to do while he's here.'

Mo cradled her mug in her hands. 'I really don't know, Tony. I mean what I said about scruples. I mean, don't you know the things the military did after the coup? I'm not surprised people are out to get Herrera.'

'Look, Mo. What this bloke may or may not have done twenty years ago is nothing to do with me or you. It's just a job, OK? All I'm doing is watching someone's back and as far as I'm concerned that's where it ends.' He stood up. 'I'm sorry I've wasted your time.'

Suddenly Mo had visions of *Cosmopolitan* and bathroom tiles. They were not pleasant. Less pleasant, even, than the thought of helping Tony with Herrera. 'What exactly,' she said, 'is it that you want me to do?'

Tony wanted Mo to go to the Chilean Exile Centre in south London. Soledad had told him of its existence, and had intimated that, short as they were of time, it would be the best place to do some prying. Mo spent the rest of the day poring through the files trying to establish who would and who wouldn't be likely to attack General Santiago Herrera. It was a fairly thankless task, and it also made harrowing reading. It soon became clear to her that just about every one of the million Chilean exiles scattered all over the world had ample reason to attack Herrera. Nothing she could find directly implicated him in any atrocities, yet it was obvious that he had had first-hand knowledge of most of the horrors that had visited his country in the past twenty years. He had, she discovered, been part of the four-man junta which had planned to run Chile temporarily after the coup – and before Pinochet had decided that his lust for power was far greater than any pretentions he may have had towards democracy. One or two of the articles Mo discovered in the files suggested that, of all Chile's military bigwigs, Herrera was the most liberal, and that he had balked at some of Pinochet's worse excesses. But by the time Mo had finished reading them she had long decided that calling Herrera a moderate was like trying to pretend a Rottweiler was actually a poodle. She almost wished she hadn't accepted the job. Yet she knew that Tony had a point: protecting Herrera's back while he was in London was not the same thing as voicing approval for past deeds in a distant country. And anyway, she wouldn't even meet the Chilean.

Later in the afternoon, having decided on her modus operandi, she picked up the phone and dialled the number of the Chilean Exile Centre in Battersea. When the phone was answered, she asked if she could speak to whoever was in charge.

A heavily accented voice answered that there was no one person in charge. What did the *señora* want?

Mo took a deep breath. 'My name is Susan Willis,' she said. 'I'm a journalist and I'm writing an article on Chile since the Christian Democrats took power. I would very much like to interview some – er – Chilean exiles who suffered under the Pinochet regime.'

On the other end of the line, the woman's voice grew friendlier as she replied, 'Ah. Well you have certainly come to the right place. Although,' she laughed a hollow laugh, 'I'm not sure that you'll find there's much difference under the Christian Democrats as far as exiles are concerned. You see—'

'I wonder,' interrupted Mo, 'if I might come along and speak to someone? Tomorrow, perhaps?' The last thing she wanted was a lecture on the phone.

'Tomorrow? Well, yes. Tomorrow at about five-thirty would be fine.'

'Oh, good. Who shall I ask for?'

'Myself. My name is Caterina Portales.'

'I'll look forward to it, Miss Portales. Thank you for your help.' Mo replaced the receiver and breathed a sigh of relief. Then she looked down at the dressing-gown she was still wearing. What sort of clothes, she thought, would someone with a name like Susan Willis wear? She went upstairs to do a little research. And as she padded into the bedroom, she silently rejoiced that Kate was away on business for two days. With any luck, she might never have to know that Mo was back in business with Tony and Harry. She would be most disapproving of that. But what she would disapprove of even more was the rush of adrenaline in Mo, the new spring in her step and the gleam in her eye that always appeared when she was back doing what she loved most: being a detective.

14

Sarah Teale's suspicions that Tony was in charge of Herrera's security were confirmed when, on the late news, she saw a clip of the General's arrival at Heathrow and the demonstration that greeted him. The newscaster made a fleeting reference to the old regime in Chile, while commenting that Herrera's visit was a private one. Huh, thought Sarah, thank God some of us know that's a load of crap. But what really interested her about the clip was the face of the man driving the first Range Rover: it was a grim-looking Tony Clark. Bingo, she thought. It's all systems go.

The following day, when Maureen was leaving her Shepherd's Bush house and adopting her Susan Willis persona, Sarah left her high-tech Butler's Wharf flat dressed in her best suit and wearing, she hoped, her most confident smile. She had spent half the night putting the final touches to her presentation, and she was pleased with it. It looked, as she had hoped, as if it would be a corker.

Encounter Productions, like every other television production company, had to sell its programme ideas to a network before it could make

157

them. Sarah, who had several times suffered bureaucratic nightmares at the hands of the BBC, had decided that she should try to sell the Chile idea to one of the independent channels. And she thought she knew which one would be most likely to be interested. But two hours after leaving her flat, she wasn't so sure. Nicky Cash, who was supposedly in charge of buying programmes at Home Counties Television, or HCTV, was doing a very good impression of someone who shouldn't be allowed out in charge of a yo-yo. It was his assistant, the vapid Jessica, who was doing all the talking, and most of what she was saying was, thought Sarah, complete drivel.

'What we're looking for,' Jessica was saying in her languid drawl, 'is gritty ideas. Something . . . something with a bit of edge.' She looked at Sarah as one would look at a backward child. 'Do you know what I mean?'

Sarah bit her lip. 'Sure.'

Jessica crossed her legs. 'Of course we need to be popular, but that doesn't mean we can't produce quality material – whatever they think in NW3.'

Sarah hadn't a clue what Jessica was talking about. 'I couldn't agree more,' she said. 'That's why I've come to you with the Chile idea.'

There was a brief silence during which Nicky Cash made a little pantomime of looking pained, tired, overworked and inundated with ideas. He dragged a weary hand through the hair which he'd spent half the morning having expensively styled. Then he rubbed his eyes to make them look bleary and, at last, looked at Sarah. 'We weren't quite sure,' he said, 'exactly what the story was.'

Either he really was a complete fool or he was a very good actor, thought Sarah. She really couldn't decide. She had had a lot of experience of being up against people like him who feigned disinterest in your programmes purely because they wanted to establish how committed you were to the idea. But Nicky Cash really took the biscuit.

Sarah took a deep breath. 'Well, Herrera's visit here is only the peg. The real story's about how Britain continues to support fascism. I mean, we were the first country since the coup to give Pinochet an entry visa and now,' here she paused for emphasis, 'we're inviting his chief torturer into the country.'

'I heard on the news,' replied Nicky, 'that he was here on a private visit.'

'I happen to know that's not true.'

'Oh?' Jessica, arching her eyebrows, managed to invest her one-word answer with seven syllables.

'Anyway,' added Nicky, 'the coup was a long time ago. It's not exactly news.'

'True. The coup just provides the background to the story. The real story, as I said, is about Britain's hypocrisy in its attitude to Chile. What I plan to do,' she said, leaning forward and warming to her theme, 'is to interview some of the Chilean exiles in this country, to hear first-hand reports from the thousands of families who are still looking for relatives who were tortured and then disappeared.'

Nicky Cash nodded. 'Sure. Like the film *Missing*, right?' Sarah nodded. At last he appeared to be showing genuine interest. Jessica, on the other hand, was clicking her tongue and inspecting her immaculate nail-varnish.

'*But*,' continued Sarah, 'the real power of the story is that while we've been sheltering these exiles and publicly decrying the brutal regime in Chile, we've been happily negotiating arms deals with them and enlisting their help in winning our wars.'

'Oh, I really don't think that's the case,' said Jessica. 'Chile? Helping *us*?' She looked pityingly at Sarah. 'I really think you must be mistaken.'

Sarah stared at her with barely concealed irritation. 'I'm not wrong. I'm not wrong at all.' And then she leaned forward and regaled Nicky and Jessica with the true story of the Falklands War, the arms to Iraq deal, and the real reason for General Santiago Herrera's visit to Britain.

Nearly half an hour later, she finished her impassioned speech and still couldn't decide if Nicky Cash was interested. He had, at least, stopped playing with his hair and even Jessica had given up examining her hands, but both of them were still lingering on the bored side of cautious.

'So how,' said Nicky at last, 'are you going to corroborate this information? It's pretty powerful stuff.' Sarah looked at him, hoping he couldn't detect the increase in her heartbeat. 'I'm afraid I can't reveal my sources re the collaboration between the two Governments, but I *can* substantiate my information. And as for Herrera, I can get straight to him.'

'Oh? How?'

'I know the bodyguard who's handling security for the visit. He's already promised me unique access.'

Two minutes later Jessica ushered Sarah out of the office with an unconvincing-sounding 'We'll think it over.' Sarah wanted to hit her. Yet something kept her from being rude or from burning her boats. Somehow, she had the impression that beneath the impassive exterior, Nicky Cash was more than a little interested in her idea.

Jessica walked back into the office with a gleam in her eye that would have surprised Sarah. In her presence, the girl had seemed only half-alive. Now she was animation itself.

Nicky was still looking disinterested, but his voice betrayed a different emotion. 'What d'you think?' he asked.

'Dynamite. And just as dangerous as dynamite. Let's do it.'

15

The look of the Chilean Exile Centre matched Mo's mood. Dismal and dark, it was located in a shabby south London street, and it looked badly in need of having some money spent on it. But then, thought Mo as she drew up outside it, Chilean exiles had better things to spend their money on. Parking and locking her car, she walked briskly into the building, at the same time reminding herself of who she was. Maureen Connell usually wore trousers, leather jackets and contact lenses. Susan Willis, on the other hand, was sporting a rather dowdy dress, a mac and glasses. Earnestness, she thought, would be a suitable impression to give.

She was right. The atmosphere inside was hardly joyful. From the reception area, she was able to see several small offices, unchanged, she guessed, since the 1960s. Pinned on the walls was a variety of political and human rights posters, together with several photographs of individuals who had presumably either been tortured or gone missing. Only the clatter of ancient typewriters and the ringing of telephones gave the place a semblance of normal office life.

A harassed, serious-looking woman with a shock of unruly black hair spotted Maureen and, smiling, approached her. 'Can I help you?'

Maureen smiled back. 'I hope so. I'm Susan Willis. I spoke to Caterina Portales on the phone yesterday.'

'Oh yes.' The woman extended her hand in greeting and smiled more warmly. 'I'm Caterina. How nice to meet you.'

Maureen returned the compliment, but before she could say anything more, Caterina gestured down the corridor and, in an urgent, almost staccato voice, asked her if she knew about the debate.

'Debate? No, you didn't tell me.'

'Oh. I'm sorry. I thought I had. Come with me; it's almost over, but I think you may find it useful for your article.'

The debate, it transpired, was between a supporter of the ruling Christian Democrat Party and a member of the Revolutionary Left Movement. Caterina ushered Mo into a room at the end of the corridor where two men on a podium at the far end were addressing an audience of about thirty people. Showing Maureen to a seat at the back, Caterina then took up a position near the door.

It wasn't much of a debate: more of a hectoring session. A swarthy, over-excited man with a gaucho moustache was standing up on the podium in front of a poster of ex-President Allende. '. . . the Christian Democratic Party,' he was saying, 'has been in power for four years now, and yet members of my party, the Revolutionary Left Movement, are still being tortured and imprisoned.' Then he waved his hand in the air and raised his voice. 'Is this your idea of democracy? It's certainly not mine!'

He sat down to a few desultory claps that gave Mo the impression his speech had been too long and too impassioned to carry much weight. Then his opponent, the Christian Democrat, stood up. 'Clearly, certain parts of the police and security service have not yet been fully brought under democratic control . . .' he paused as a few members of the audience booed, '. . . but every attempt is being made to do so. It is unfair,' he added with a disapproving look at the previous speaker, 'to suggest that the Government supports the violation of human rights in any way.'

'But under the regime of the so-called Christian Democrats, what has changed?' The man with the moustache, eyes blazing with fury, jumped to his feet. 'It is Pinochetismo without Pinochet!'

The Christian Democrat spokesman, irritated beyond endurance, rounded on his opponent and exploded into a torrent of Spanish. '*Yo personalmente estuve cuatro años en la carcel!*' Now both speakers, seemingly oblivious to their audience, started yelling at each other, while their listeners broke out into arguments of their own. Maureen was finding it difficult to disguise her amusement – until Caterina, marching up to the podium, decided to interject.

'Comrades!' she shouted. 'Can we now please concentrate on the next item on the agenda? We're supposed to be co-ordinating tonight's protest for the dinner Herrera will be attending. Let's get on with that!'

Maureen, suddenly alert, looked around the room. In one corner, she noticed several placards. She didn't understand most of the words scrawled on them, but one word needed no explanation: Herrera.

This was both better and worse than Mo had expected: worse because Herrera's every movement appeared to be known to these people, and better because if the exiles were prepared to let her, a complete stranger, be privy to their plans for protests, she reckoned that those protests would be no more than that. If they were intent on violence or murder, surely they would be a little bit more circumspect? Even given the fact that this set-up looked less than professional, Mo couldn't believe they would be *that* lax. She stole a quick glance at Caterina, who was now surrounded by people waving their banners and placards. Hoping that her absence would not be noticed for a few minutes, she hurried out of the room and out of the building. Finding a phone box was foremost on her agenda.

She found one almost opposite the Exile head-quarters and, without further ado, dialled Tony's mobile. She looked at her watch: it was nearly seven o'clock. Tony would, she reckoned, already be en route for the dinner.

He answered immediately – and almost bit her head off when she told him the news. 'What'll you do now?' asked Maureen.

'Return to the house, I guess.'

'Oh.'

After Maureen replaced the phone, Tony turned to Herrera, resplendent in a dinner jacket in the back seat of the Range Rover, and told him the news. Herrera was unmoved. 'Mr Clark,' he said icily, 'it takes a good deal more than a bunch of long-hairs to frighten me off. Now carry on!'

Tony, furious but powerless in the face of his employer's command, carried on.

Maureen, too, carried on with her work, returning straight away to the Exile Centre. As she did so, several of the protesters filed out of the building, many of them with the placards carrying anti-fascist slogans in both English and Spanish. Edging her way past them, Mo headed once more towards the meeting room in the hope that Caterina Portales would still be there.

She was – but it was the person she was talking to who caused Mo to freeze in her tracks. It was Sarah Teale. Putting a hand to her mouth in horror, Mo tried to edge away discreetly. She was too late: Caterina had already spotted her. 'Susan!' she exclaimed.

Feeling slightly sick, Mo smiled weakly and turned to the two women. Sarah, whose initial smile of recognition was wiped off her face by her confusion over Caterina's greeting, looked uncertainly at her as Caterina began to introduce them. 'Susan, this is Sarah Teale. She's making a film about Herrera. And Sarah, this is the journalist Susan Willis. She's writing an article about our work here at the centre.'

She smiled at the two women and added, with undisguised enthusiasm. 'I can't tell you,' she continued, 'how pleased we are about this. Media coverage in print *and* on the television! I don't think we've ever had such exposure: it'll do our cause a great deal of good.'

Sarah and Mo, both confused and embarrassed, hesitated and then shook hands. 'It's nice to meet you,' said Sarah. 'I've . . . I've always enjoyed your work.'

Mo grinned. 'And I yours.' What the hell, she thought, is this all about? Then she remembered why she had had a sense of *déja vu* when Tony had come to discuss this job: it had been Sarah, ages ago, who had talked to her about Chile. So, she mused, here we all are. With vested interests. Again. She wondered if Tony knew about Sarah's film. She doubted that he did: his job was to keep people away from Herrera, not arrange interviews with mud-slinging journalists, no matter how much he fancied them. 'We must,' she continued, 'meet up properly to . . . er, to discuss our respective projects.'

'That,' said Sarah with a pointed look, 'would be a very good idea.'

They met, in fact, half an hour later as they emerged from the building after their respective talks with different people. 'Well, this *is* a surprise,' said Mo. 'Does Tony know about this latest venture of yours?'

Sarah feigned surprise. 'No. Why should he?'

'Because he's protecting Herrera while he's here. I doubt he'll be ecstatic when he finds out you're trying to get at him.'

'Get to him, Mo. Not at him. All I want is to ask him a few questions.'

'You'll be lucky.'

'That's what I'm hoping I'll be.' She paused and

looked slyly at Mo before continuing. 'You wouldn't, by any chance, like to arrange an interview with me?'

'No, I wouldn't. I've got nothing to do with Herrera and I don't want to. All I'm doing is trying to find out where the protesters are getting their information from and what they're planning next.'

'They're getting it, I believe, from the embassy. I've been told it leaks like a sieve. And as for what's going to happen next, that's what I intend to find out.'

'How?'

'By going to the banqueting hall to tackle Herrera.'

'Tony'll love that.'

'Well, that's just too bad.' Sarah paused and then, with renewed earnestness, asked Maureen if she had any idea what sort of man Herrera really was.

'No, Sarah, I don't. And I don't think I want to know.'

'Hmm. It just surprises me that you – and even Tony for that matter – would accept a job like this.' She looked at Mo. 'Herrera was Pinochet's right-hand man, you know. He was also the chief of Chile's secret police.'

'Look, Sarah, it's just a job. I'm not responsible for what Herrera did – and I'm not saying I approve, either. Tony's just watching his back for a week, and that's the start and finish of it. Anyway,' she added, 'you may disapprove all you like, but it does strikes me as rather convenient for you that Tony's doing this job.'

'You mean you reckon Tony'll let me have access to Herrera?'

'No. But at least he won't punch you in the face when you try to get to him.'

Sarah laughed. 'Oh well, I guess that's something.' Then she looked at her watch. 'Look, Mo, or should I say Susan? I've got to get going if I'm going to try to catch Herrera outside this dinner. Wish me luck.'

Mo grinned. 'I'm not sure that I should. I think I should regard you as the enemy.'

Sarah was suddenly all seriousness. 'When I'm finished with this programme, Mo, then we'll really know who the enemy is. I think it might surprise you.'

But what would have surprised Mo was that two men in a parked car were taking an unusual interest in the two women. What would have surprised her even more was that they had followed her earlier in the day from her home to south London. And it would be Sarah's turn to be surprised if she had any idea, when she parted company with Mo, that they had begun to follow her.

16

Mo's phone call and Herrera's subsequent refusal to withdraw from the dinner had really riled Tony. From the word go this job had been a nightmare – and it certainly wasn't getting any better. Both Herrera and his wife were at once distant and demanding, the Chilean bodyguards insisted on parading all over the place with their weapons in full view, and Osvaldo del Canto had made it perfectly clear that he regarded Tony as an amateur. Worse, Soledad, for all her apparent efficiency and professionalism, didn't seem the least bit perturbed that the likelihood of Herrera being attacked was increasing. And now, approaching the banqueting hall, Tony noted with despair that the protesters were already lined up outside the building. He prepared himself for the worst.

The Chilean bodyguards, he was gratified to see, leaped out of the vehicles the moment they stopped. At the same time the crowd, identifying Herrera, shouted and surged forward. A terrific, undignified scrum developed as the Chileans, Harry and Tony all tried to shield the General and his wife from the angry mob and to usher them into the banqueting hall as quickly as possible. As they edged forward, Tony felt someone pressing up against him and, irritated and flustered, turned round. It took a moment for him to register that he was staring into the face of Sarah Teale. She had a microphone in her hand and, behind her, a film crew at the ready.

'You?' he exclaimed rudely. 'What the hell are you doing here?'

'I could,' replied Sarah, 'ask the same of you. But no wonder you wouldn't tell me the identity of your Chilean.' Tony couldn't decide whether or not she was serious as she added: 'You should be ashamed of yourself, Tony.' Then, taking advantage of his momentary hesitation, she slipped past him and started firing questions at Herrera. 'General Herrera how do you answer allegations that while you were head of the Chilean secret police, hundreds of people were tortured and murdered?'

But General Herrera, unsurprisingly, chose not to answer the allegations. Nor did he open his mouth when Sarah asked him why Chile had denied helping Britain in the Falklands War. And he remained stoically silent as she asked him about Britain laundering arms for Iraq through his country. Sarah had to shout her last question as, enraged by her interruption, his guards pushed her roughly back into the body of the crowd. Tony, now helping Doña Hilda up the steps to the building, compressed his lips in anger and shook his head in disbelief. Yet again, he was trying to get emotionally involved with a woman who was jeopardising his career. He

171

seemed to attract them like a magnet.

Once in the banqueting hall, the General regained his composure and, with Doña Hilda on his arm, walked sedately towards the little group who were waiting for them at the entrance. The man at the front, the managing director of the arms company with whom Herrera was negotiating, stepped forward to greet him and soon the protesters were forgotten as the Herreras became the centre of an altogether more pleasant kind of attention. Even Doña Hilda started to smile as she was ushered to her seat at the high table. This, she thought, was more like it. This was how Lucia Pinochet must have been treated. With Soledad beside her to act as interpreter, and Miles Courtenay, the managing director, on the other, she settled down to enjoy her evening.

There was no such settling down, however, for Harry and Tony. Although they were dressed in dinner jackets as befitted the occasion, they were not to be seated at dinner. Their job was to patrol the room as unobtrusively as possible, to make sure that everything ran smoothly and that there were no uninvited guests. But as he surveyed the room from a vantage point in the corner, Tony suddenly did a double-take. At a table of eight near the centre of the room was a man he certainly had not expected to see. He knew him so well he even recognised him from behind: from the thick-set shoulders and the thinning dark hair there was no mistaking that one of the guests – and Tony didn't doubt for a moment that he had a legitimate invitation – was John Deakin. Harry shrugged. He knew Deakin better than most people and wasn't remotely surprised that the man should turn up at an occasion like this. The more sensitive the project, the more likely he was to be there. Tony, for about the first time in his life, was actually glad to see Deakin: he was sure his ex-boss had no idea he was in charge of Herrera's personal security, and was rather looking forward to be able to tell him so.

His chance came sooner than he expected. Deakin must have had eyes in the back of his head for, almost as soon as Tony removed himself to a better viewing-station on the balcony above, Deakin appeared next to him.

'Tony, how are you?'

Startled by the unexpected yet familiar quiet, authoritative voice, Tony swung round. Deakin, with one hand holding the inevitable cigarette and the other smoothing the already immaculate lapel of his dinner-jacket, smiled his cryptic smile.

'I'm fine,' said Tony, annoyed that he had lost the initiative. 'What on earth are you doing here?'

Deakin shrugged. 'Oh, just meeting a few people, you know.' Then he smiled again. 'But I must say I'm glad to see you're keeping busy.' He gestured to the throng of diners beneath them. 'A considerable contract you've got yourself here.' Tony, being Tony, couldn't help but look inordinately pleased wih himself. Then, in what he hoped was a nonchalant, 'it happens every day' tone, he shrugged and replied. 'Yeah, well, I think people realise that I'm a safe pair of hands.' He paused, letting the implication that he was no longer reliant on Deakin sink in.

But Deakin, being Deakin, immediately took the wind out of his sails. 'I heard a rumour,' he said, 'that might interest you. Someone was offering big money for a contract.'

Tony looked suddenly wary. 'On who?'

'On a visiting South American. A military man.'

Tony was now feeling extremely uneasy. 'When did you hear this?'

'Oh, a few weeks ago.' Again Deakin smiled. 'I would have told you sooner, but then you hadn't told me what you were up to.' This time it was he who stopped to let the implication sink in. Don't, ran the subtext of his words, keep me uninformed about your movements. I have, after all, got my finger in every pie.

But before Tony had a chance to think of a suitable reply, Deakin turned round and headed towards the staircase. Raising a hand in farewell, he announced that he'd better get back to the other guests.

Tony, alone on the balcony, was furious. He had no idea whether or not Deakin was serious about the threat, but he'd certainly succeeded in alarming him. Great, he thought, I've probably got a contract killer in the room. He leaned on the balustrade and looked down. There were probably over a hundred people in the hall. Impossible to search them; impossible to know if there was a lethal little hand-gun at large. He rolled his eyes. This evening, he thought, is going to be horrific.

Had Tony been able to witness what had just happened behind the scenes, he would have realised that the horrors had already begun. Ten minutes earlier, in the storage area beside the kitchens, two Latin-looking waiters had cautiously and quietly made their way towards a grubby window that gave on to a small courtyard at the back of the building. After ascertaining that no one was watching, they deftly opened the window and beckoned to a shadowy figure outside. The figure approached, revealing itself to be a woman of about sixty, dark-haired and plump. At first sight she looked not unlike Hilda Herrera. Closer up, however, it became evident that this woman had led an entirely different sort of life – a life of hard work and little reward. Her face was heavily lined, her hands were chafed and her nails chewed to the quick. But it was her eyes that revealed the most; they spoke not of hardship but of tragedy, not of resignation but of bitterness. Yet there was also a fire in them, and as the two men helped her through the window, that fire brightened and gave her a look almost of fanaticism. She looked like a woman bent on a task from which nothing would deter her.

Once inside, she smiled at the waiters and they exchanged a few brief words in Spanish. Then one of the men gave her a bundle of clothes and, with a smile of thanks, she began to divest herself of the drab skirt and blouse she had been wearing. Two minutes later, Violetta Tapia, dressed as a waitress, was ready for business.

Nobody paid much attention to Violetta as she mingled with the rest of the staff. The servery was frenetically busy as the waiting staff prepared to deliver one hundred soufflés to the guests in the banqueting hall. The fact that the staff were multi-ethnic helped Violetta to blend in unobtrusively, and as a bevy of waitresses hurried into the hall,

Violetta tagged along behind. But where the others were carrying soufflés, Violetta was only holding a napkin: a very bulky-looking napkin.

Miles Courtenay was in the middle of making a welcoming speech as Violetta approached. 'Ladies and gentlemen,' he was saying, 'I'm sure you will all want to join me in offering a warm welcome to our special guests this evening, General and Señora Herrera.' He bestowed his most dazzling smile on the Chilean couple and then continued, 'What a pleasure it is to have such friends of our industry – and indeed of Britain itself – amongst us . . .' Here the audience interrupted him with cheers and cries of 'Hear, hear!' Smiling even more broadly, glad that the evening looked like being a success despite the continued presence of the protesters outside, he pressed on: 'As many of you know, our company has had a long and fruitful relationship with the Chilean armed forces, and the joint ventures we have mounted during that time have resulted in some of the most advanced, and indeed most cost-effective systems we have produced.'

He beamed at the assembled guests and reflected, not for the first time, how wise his company was to ban the press from functions such a this. People got unnecessarily twitchy about arms deals; they seldom, he thought, stopped to think what a boost they were for the economy. And the press could get awfully boring about Chile's past human rights record.

As he smiled he noticed out of the corner of his eye that the waiting staff were emerging from the kitchen. He bent immediately to his notes and continued with his speech. It wouldn't do, his wife had told him, to keep the soufflé waiting.

A few yards away from him, Harry Naylor had also noticed the arrival of the staff, and of one individual in particular. The small, dark woman who was rapidly approaching the top table wasn't, he saw, carrying any food. She was, however, carrying something concealed under a napkin. She was also staring at Herrera with an expression of pure hatred. In an instant, Harry was moving towards her. As her own pace quickened, he flung himself at her, knocking her to the ground.

At that point, all the bodyguards acted instinctively and as one. Tony threw himself between the now-screaming woman and Herrera, noting with relief that Osvaldo del Canto was covering him. The three other guards piled into the mêlée on the floor just as Harry reached for the gun the woman was hiding under the napkin. But there was no gun. The object with which the woman had been going to threaten Herrera was nothing more than an old black and white photograph of a young girl. Shocked and surprised, Harry let go of her arm. Her eyes blazing with fury, Violetta struggled to her feet and started shouting at Herrera. '*Donde está mi hija?*' she screamed. 'Where is my daughter? Where is my daughter?'

As a stunned silence reigned in the room, the Chilean guards swept the woman off her feet again and, none too gently, started to drag her out of the hall. But her final words hung ominously in the room. Straining to turn her neck, she glared once more at the embarrassed Herrera and screamed again. 'This man killed my daughter! Where is my daughter?' Then, managing to wrench a hand free from her captors, she pointed an accusatory finger at the General. '*Asesino! Asesino!*'

The strength of her words and the hatred with which they were uttered was matched only by the highly audible slap as one of the guards forcibly quietened her.

Chaos dominated the hall. Miles Courtenay was, for the first time, completely lost for words. Doña Hilda was screaming blue murder and then everybody else started talking at once. Tony turned to Herrera. 'Are you all right?'

Herrera, clearly shaken, nodded. Then, as the buzz died down, Tony raced off after the guards. Something told him that they would be treating the woman as if she had tried to assassinate Herrera rather than just shove a photograph under his nose. His worse suspicions were confirmed when he found them in the filthy courtyard through which Violetta had entered. She was lying on the ground with blood all over her face, screaming in terror and agony as the three bodyguards tried to beat the living daylights out of her. Luís had her trapped with her arms behind her back, Jorge was punching her in the face while Antonio, screaming obscenities, was kicking her stomach.

Horrified, Tony felt a tightening in his lower stomach as he fought back the desire to vomit. He had never in his life expected to see three fully grown young men attack a frail old lady with such appalling ferocity.

'You animals!' he yelled as he joined in the fray, flooring Jorge with one well-aimed punch. 'You bloody animals! You can't do that here, she's an old woman! You *can't do that here*!' Still holding the advantage of surprise, he landed another punch in Luís's guts and the man doubled over in agony. But Antonio, quick to gather his wits, was on to him in a flash and held him in a vice-like neck-hold. Violetta, still screaming, picked herself up and ran towards the doorway to the service area and collided with a panting Harry. Righting himself and steadying the terrified woman, Harry, who, unlike Tony, had earned the grudging respect of the Chileans, managed to pull the struggling men apart. Tony, dishevelled and disgusted, stood and glared at the guards as, full of contempt, they grouped together. Luís, brushing his dirty clothes and soothing his affronted machismo, started laughing derisively at Tony. '*Concha de su madre*!' he scoffed. Harry, guessing correctly that Tony was not prepared to be insulted, quickly restrained his boss's instinctive reaction.

'Come on, Guv,' he urged gently. 'Leave it alone.'

Tony glared at him, and then back at the guards. But, already shrugging off the incident, they were heading back into the building.

Soledad, who had followed hot on Harry's heels, was trying to comfort the still hysterical Violetta. She looked up at Harry. 'I think we'd better get her to hospital. She's quite badly hurt.'

Tony bit his lip and looked at the victim. She would, he conceded, have to have medical treatment. She was a mess. But Tony also had other responsibilities. 'We can't, take her out the front,' he said to Soledad. 'The other protesters are still there and if they see her, there'll be a full-scale riot.'

Soledad nodded. 'True. I'll take her out the back. You two stay with the General.'

This time Tony nodded. 'Fine. You've got my mobile number, haven't you? Let me know which hospital you're taking her to. The least I can do is apologise.'

He supposed he ought also to apologise to Herrera, yet he couldn't bring himself to do so. Ultimately responsible for the General's security he might have been, but he was so disgusted by the performance of the Chilean bodyguards that he felt Herrera should be apologising to him for importing wild animals into the country. In any event, the rest of the dinner passed without incident and, three hours later, the little convoy of Range Rovers was again heading through Berkshire towards the safe house.

In the back of Tony's vehicle, Doña Herrera was giving her husband a hard time about their disastrous evening. The Pinochets, ran her argument, would not have been subjected to such indignities. They would have had *proper* security arrangements. Herrera's weary, disinterested responses indicated that he had heard this sort of thing many times before. The atmosphere in the front of the car was no better. In the passenger seat, del Canto sat impassively, staring straight ahead. Although he had not been part of the fight in the courtyard, he had heard all about it, and it was clear that his sympathies did not lie with Tony. Tony himself was still very upset about the violent incident. At least Soledad had called from Charing Cross Hospital to say that the woman, Violetta Tapia, was all right. He was glad when he was able to turn into the gates of the safe house and speed up the drive.

Harry's vehicle, drawing up behind Tony's, disgorged the Chilean guards who, without even glancing in Tony's direction, filed into the house behind the Herreras.

Tony gave Harry an old-fashioned look. 'Everything OK?'

Harry grinned lopsidedly. 'OK' was not the expression he would have chosen to describe the atmosphere in the car he had been driving. He had lost his rapport with the Chilean guards and, during the journey from the banqueting hall, they had made no bones about the fact that they now regarded both Harry and Tony as wimps. 'Yeah,' he replied to Tony, 'just fine.'

'Good. I'm going to drop in at the hospital. Soledad reckons the woman will be all right, but I think it would be the done thing to pay her a visit. Can you keep an eye on things here?'

'No problem.'

'You'd better take this,' finished Tony. He handed the security system arming key to Harry and, without further ado, got back into the Range Rover and headed back to London.

Much of his uncharacteristic quietness during the latter part of the evening had been due to the qualms Tony was now beginning to have regarding the whole Herrera business. He had meant what he said to Mo about a job being a job, but now that he had first-hand experience of the people and methods the Pinochet regime had employed, he was not so sure. He had also been slightly

181

thrown by the vehemence and depth of feeling behind Sarah's questions to Herrera as he had entered the banqueting hall. Tony knew that the extent of the Chilean involvement in the Falklands War had never been properly revealed by either side, no doubt because Britain would have had to reveal just how heavily involved it was in arms deals with Chile. But he hadn't known about laundering arms to Iraq through Chile. Now that the whole Gulf War scenario was increasingly becoming a deep embarrassment to Her Majesty's Government, the last thing they would want revealed would be yet more hypocrisy regarding Chile. Their public stance against that country's appalling human rights record would soon be revealed as the empty and insincere gesture it most surely was.

Tony, furthermore, had been alarmed by his chance encounter with John Deakin. It hadn't been the man's hint that there was a contract out on Herrera that had bothered him so much as his actual presence at the dinner. Tony knew far too much about Deakin's activities to be led into thinking that his attendance had been mere coincidence. He reckoned that Deakin had been sent by the security services to keep an eye on things. And one of the things he was sure to have had his beady eye on was Sarah Teale's arrival with a film crew. The security services wouldn't want a film about Herrera: it would be, at the very least, an embarrassment. And at the very worst, it could spark off a major scandal.

Tony himself didn't want Sarah poking her nose into the Herrera affair, but for quite different reasons. While he would, in theory, welcome any scandal a documentary might provoke, the fact was that he could not help, in a minor way, becoming involved in it. And from the point of view of any further Government contracts, he would be finished career-wise. While he wasn't yet romantically involved with Sarah Teale, it wouldn't take long for the powers that be to suspect that he had been feeding her with information.

As he drove into the forecourt of the Charing Cross Hospital, Tony reflected that his position was, putting it mildly, unenviable. He was up shit creek and his paddle had disappeared downstream. All he wanted was for the Herrera job to be over with as quickly as possible, and with as little fuss as possible. And that meant trying to hush up the unfortunate affair of Violetta Tapia.

The first person he saw after he entered the waiting area of the Accident and Emergency Department was Sarah. He groaned audibly as he saw her walking through the swing doors with a cameraman behind her. The nurse who caught sight of Sarah at the same time was, however, much more vocal.

'You can't,' she shouted, 'bring a camera in here!'

Sarah, who had suspected as much, quickly conferred with the hapless cameraman. He then departed as she marched purposefully into the room. If she was surprised to see Tony she didn't show it. Walking straight up to him, she asked him where Violetta was.

'The doctor's seeing her,' he replied. 'She's all right.'

Sarah evidently thought this rather an under-statement. 'Well, at least you scraped her up off the ground and got her into a hospital. I don't imagine *that* was in your contract.'

Tony wasn't in the mood for sarcasm. He ran a weary hand through his hair and looked at Sarah in exasperation. 'I really haven't got time for this, you know.'

But Sarah was not to be deflected. 'These people are murderers, Tony! They torture and kill people, and you're *working* for them!'

Tony lost his temper. 'So I'm the only one profiting from all this, am I? You've got a nice little story, haven't you? And at the end of the day that's what pays your mortgage, so don't give me this shit!'

Sarah looked rather taken aback. 'It's com-pletely different,' she said quietly.

'Oh, is it? The only difference is that I don't have the luxury of kidding myself that I'm doing something "worthwhile". We've both got our snouts in the same trough.'

Now it was Sarah who lost her temper. 'Herrera,' she shouted, 'or one of his henchmen, killed that woman's daughter!'

Tony glared at her. 'And bursting into that dinner changes any of that, does it? I bet you really tried to persuade her not to do it, didn't you? I bet you begged her not to go through with it.'

'Oh, don't be so silly,' snapped Sarah. 'I had nothing to do with her. Anyway, her protest is all she has. Of course I wasn't going to stop her.'

'Yeah, well her protest has cost her twelve

184

stitches in her face – and nothing has changed.' He turned on his heel. 'Try thinking about that when you're picking up your BAFTA Award.' With that, he stomped off out of the hospital, leaving Sarah looking furious, dejected – and thoughtful.

Sarah did not remain downcast for long. As usual when emotional trauma threatened, she became even more absorbed in her work. And Sarah Teale the television producer had an extra card up her sleeve.

In her years as a producer, Sarah had met many people and made a point of keeping in touch with those she suspected would go places. One of these had been a junior member of the Opposition party who, unlike the pompous Jeremy Taylor, had succeeded in seducing her. She hadn't, in truth, tried to deflect his advances. But while their sexual relationship had fizzled out some years ago, they had still kept in touch. She was heartily glad they had, because Bob Wilkinson had risen through the ranks and had recently been appointed to the board which was heading the arms to Iraq inquiry. If anybody could find out about Chile's involvement in the affair, it would be Bob. Sarah, of course, knew that there was no such thing as a free lunch and that if she was going to persuade Bob to part with classified information she would have to give something in return. It hadn't taken her long to establish what she had to give.

Tony, on the other hand, was not in a much better mood when, just before midnight, he arrived back at the safe house. Harry, on duty at the video

185

monitor, saw him approaching and went to let him in.

Tony spoke before Harry had a chance to say anything. 'Guess who I ran into at the hospital?'

'General Pinochet?' As soon as he had said it, Harry realised his little joke wasn't exactly in the best possible taste.

Tony just glared at him. 'Sarah.'

'Sarah?'

'Sarah Teale. Intrepid maker of documentaries that rock the establishment. She's certainly trying her best to rock this establishment, that's for sure.'

'Oh? How?'

'Well, you heard the questions she asked Herrera before the banquet? Now she's got her claws into that poor Violetta Tapia woman. It'll make a very interesting piece of film. A very damaging one – and we'll be in it.'

Harry wasn't convinced. 'Look, Guv, I mean . . . is this really such a big deal? I mean, the guy's just some jumped-up thug. I can't see why a documentary about him will cause such stink.'

'That's because the documentary's not just about him. I think she's going for the works: the real story of torture and killing in Chile; the Falklands War and then Britain laundering arms through Chile. It's not exactly a fairy tale for kids. You saw,' he added, 'what those boys did to that Tapia woman. Imagine what they'd do to someone who *really* got their goat.'

'I don't,' replied Harry firmly, 'think I'm capable of imagining.'

'Mmm. Talking of which, how are the bully-boys?'

186

'Not speaking.'

'Well, at least that's an improvement.' Tony smiled grimly and patted Harry on the shoulder. 'I'm going to call Mo and let her know what's going on. You go and get some rest.'

'Sure.' Then, just as he was walking off, Harry turned back as he remembered something. 'Oh, by the way, I nearly forgot. The General wants to see you. He's in the lounge.'

A look of slight trepidation passed across Tony's face. 'Oh. Did he say what it was about?'

'No.'

'Oh.' Reluctantly, Tony made his way through the hall and paused for a second outside the lounge door. Then, squaring his shoulders, he entered the room.

Herrera was sitting in an armchair near the fire, reading a newspaper. He looked up and smiled as Tony closed the door behind him. 'Mr Clark.'

'You wanted,' said Tony, 'to see me?'

Herrera put down his newspaper and gestured at the large glass of brandy on the table. 'Yes, I do. Why don't you sit down and have a drink?'

Tony moved not a muscle. 'It's all right. I'm fine, thanks.'

Herrera, whose polite offers were normally recognised as the commands they actually were, was rather annoyed. He tried another smile. 'Look, I just wanted to apologise to you on behalf of my staff for . . . for the unfortunate incident this evening with the woman.' He grimaced in distaste. 'It was very unprofessional of my men to behave in such a way, and they will be disciplined.'

Tony looked, without expression, at the General.

'I hope,' he continued, 'that we can put the whole thing in the past.'

Tony shrugged. 'Sure.'

'Good. Well, now would you at least sit with me for a while? I would enjoy talking with you.'

'I've got things to do,' replied Tony rudely.

Herrera looked at him for a moment, weighing up his response. 'You know,' he said eventually, 'the feeling of contempt you have for me and my men is misplaced.'

'Is it really? I think beating the shit out of old women is pretty contemptible.'

Herrera, for the first time in their encounter, looked angry. 'No doubt you have heard that I have been involved in . . . certain activities that you find distasteful, abhorrent even. You can't, I daresay, imagine how any civilized man could contemplate such acts?'

Tony looked him straight in the eye. 'I don't think there's any excuse for what you've done.'

Herrera tried again. 'You're an intelligent man, Mr Clark. Surely you can imagine circumstances in which you, too, would carry out such acts?'

Tony remained mute and continued looking him straight in the eye.

'There's nothing,' continued the General with an expansive wave of the hand, 'that I would not do to protect my country. However unpleasant it may have been, I did my duty.'

Tony's lip curled in disgust. 'Your duty?'

'Yes, my duty as a soldier. Twenty-two years ago the Soviets were poised to overrun the whole of South America, and if it hadn't been for men like me they would have done so.' His face flushed with emotion, he glared at Tony. 'The Cold War,' he spat, 'wasn't fought in Europe, it was fought in the back-streets and shanty towns of countries like Chile. *We*,' he jabbed at his chest, 'were the front line.'

Now Tony couldn't contain his anger. He had a horrible vision of Goebbels, of Beria, and of other feared secret police chiefs who had countenanced massacre and then tried to justify it. His eyes were like ice as he replied. 'You should never have been allowed into this country.'

Herrera actually smiled. 'I should have been welcomed here like a hero, not treated like a leper.' Then he laughed the same scoffing laugh that his guards had directed towards Tony earlier in the evening. 'As if Britain played no part in the dirty business! You are a nation of hypocrites, Mr Clark. It is thanks to me, and to people like me, that you have your freedom. And I think,' he added archly, 'you know exactly what I'm talking about.' Then he reached for his glass. 'Now, if you don't mind, I would like to finish my brandy.'

17

'So what exactly,' asked the man at the head of the table, 'is this all about?' His voice, like his expression, betrayed his irritation. He disliked being called to an emergency evening meeting by some jittery back-room boys from MI5.

The man on his left, aware that he was being given the evil eye, crossed his legs and, as was his habit when he was working up to dropping a bombshell, polished one already gleaming brogue on a pinstriped trouser leg. Then he coughed and looked to his right. 'Have you, er, heard of Tony Clark? He used to be with the CIB.'

If he had hoped to get a positive reaction from that, he was wrong. Instead he found himself on the end of a withering look and a 'Tony who?'

'Tony Clark. He used to be Detective Superintendent until he fell foul of my department. Shame he had to go – apparently he was pretty bloody good. Still, it was either him or Angela Barrett, and we couldn't afford to blow her wide open.'

'Ah.' Realisation dawned on the imposing figure at the head of the table. 'That one. Yes, I remember. Ruffled a few feathers in his time.' He paused and scratched his cheek reflectively. 'What's he up to now?'

'He's in charge of General Herrera's security.'

The older man reacted with lightning speed. 'General Herrera's visit has nothing to do with the Government. Nothing. It's a private visit.' He started to get to his feet. 'Now, if the employment of some two-bit ex-copper is the only reason for this meeting then I'm afraid you've wasted your time.' He looked pointedly at his watch. 'And mine. I have to get back to Downing Street.'

The man on his right, hitherto silent, suddenly spoke. 'With all due respect, sir, Tony Clark is just part of an equation.' He paused. 'An equation that *does* concern the Government.'

'Oh?'

'Yes. Clark himself isn't the problem. Henry Goode at the FO rates him highly and we have a, um, source called Deakin who says he's a chippy bastard but always does the job.'

'So what *is* the problem? Get on with it, man.'

But it was the other man who got on with it. 'The problem is that Clark is . . . I believe the expression is "dating" a woman who has a habit of sticking her nose in where it's not wanted. A woman who just happens to be quite a high-powered TV producer.'

'And?'

'And she's very interested in Herrera. She's trying to make a documentary on him, and on Chile's relations with Britain.'

'Oh?' For the first time the man who claimed he was in a hurry began to show interest. 'And you think Clark may be feeding her information?'

'Unlikely. I don't think he knows anything about

191

Herrera and our . . . relations with Chile. But this woman, I guarantee you, will do her damnedest to find out. She's already been nosing around the Chilean Exile Centre. And she pushed her wretched cameras in front of Herrera's nose at that banquet.'

'And furthermore,' interjected his colleague, 'she's very thick with Clark's ex-side-kick, a woman called Maureen Connell. Connell's well known for her left-wing views and you can bet on it that she's using her not inconsiderable investigative skills to help Sarah Teale.'

'Who?'

'Sarah Teale. The TV producer.'

The man at the head of the table continued to frown. 'Teale . . . an unusual name. It also rings a bell.'

The two men flanking him looked at each other. 'We thought it might,' said the brogue-polisher. 'Her brother was – is – David Teale.'

Again the frown. 'Yes . . . that *does* ring a bell. Who is he?'

'Nobody very much. He might have been, were it not for the fact that he was run down by a car fourteen years ago and crippled for life. The driver,' he added almost nonchalantly, 'was never indicted.'

The man at the head of the table went suddenly white. Then, equally suddenly, a deep flush coloured his already bilious countenance and his Adam's apple quivered slightly. If he was going to reply, he quickly thought the better of it and remained silent until he had composed himself. 'Yes,' he said at length, 'I'd heard that the family

192

wasn't satisfied with the ... outcome.' Then he appeared to remember something else. 'Is Sarah Teale the one we've had trouble with before?'

'Yes.'

'The Brighton bombing?'

'Yes.'

'Ah.' Again he paused for reflection. 'She seems to have something against the Government, doesn't she?'

'You could say that, sir.'

'So she might find out something about our relations with Chile and then get the wrong end of the stick, eh?' His previous irritated and supercilious manner had completely evaporated. Now he was in his 'we're all boys together' mode, and he was making rather heavy weather of it. The realisation that these men from MI5 knew as much as he did about events that happened years ago was deeply embarrassing to him; and it was yet another reminder of the fact that, when it came to matters of who protects whom, the security services were way ahead of the Government – and were calling all the shots. 'We wouldn't want that, would we?' he continued in his unconvincingly jocular manner.

'Indeed not.'

Downing Street, it was clear, would have to wait. 'So she has to be persuaded that this documentary isn't a good idea. Clark, you say, isn't a problem, but this Connell woman might be?'

'Well . . .'

'You boys have anything up your sleeves on her?'

The men from MI5 again looked at each other, barely concealing their distaste for their companion. 'Well,' said one, 'we know, of course, that she's a lesbian, but —'

'Perfect! Perfect! A few words in the right ears and she'll never be employed again.'

'But she's out of the closet. She's living with another woman. And anyway, with all due respect, sir, homosexuality is no longer a crime.'

'No, but it's. . . well it's . . .' he trailed off, realising that his opinions on homosexuality, strong though they were, were not going to win him any points here.

'I don't think,' said the man with the brogues, 'that Connell is the problem, either. She's only a bit player in this. Teale's the dangerous one.'

Alarm registered on the features of the man at the head of the table. 'I trust you realise, gentlemen, that we cannot afford to be seen to be getting in her way? If she is to be stopped, it must be done discreetly.' He laughed in an attempt to bolster camaraderie. 'Freedom of speech, you know, is quite the thing nowadays. Some people,' he added to himself, 'still believe in it. Anyway, I really don't think we can be seen to be interfering in her activities. Not, that is, overtly.'

'Quite. We thought you'd say that. That's why we thought we'd attack it from the other direction.'

'The other direction?'

'Yes. The people she's trying to interest in her documentary. Home Counties TV.'

'Oh.' HCTV was well known for its less than tolerant attitude towards the Government. Then the man who had already gone through various stages of irritation, impatience and embarrassment looked angrily to either side of him. 'Well, why on earth do you need me to help you with this? You know perfectly well that you have the authorisation to walk straight into HCTV and tell them that they would be in breach of national security if they went anywhere near Teale's documentary. Come on, gentlemen, you know how to put the frighteners on people like that. It's your job, for heaven's sake!'

The man on his left had long stopped polishing his shoes. He was now thoroughly enjoying embarrassing the man they had called to this meeting. 'We know that, sir, but there's another little problem.'

'And what's that?'

'Teale has another contact. A contact in Parliament.'

There was a brief yet loaded silence.

'Who?'

'He's only a junior Opposition member, and of course he's quite new so he's not been privy to any. . . historical information directly concerning the Teale case, but as regards anything to do with Chile he *is* on the arms to Iraq inquiry and —'

'Oh God . . . him?'

'Yes. Him.'

'And that's why you need me?'

'Yes, sir. We would like to request that he is removed from office immediately. It would, I think, be in your own best interests.'

The man at the head of the table shot both his companions a furious look, pushed back his chair, and stood up. 'Consider it done,' he said curtly.

195

Then, realising that, once again, MI5 had averted potential disaster, he mumbled a thank you. 'I'm very grateful,' he managed to say, 'that you have informed me of this. I can assure you that your diligence won't go unrewarded.'

As he left the room, the men from MI5 looked at each other and grinned. They had already had their reward. The power of their organisation had, yet again, been proven and consolidated.

18

The next day two things happened which would have interested Tony a great deal if he had got to hear about them at the time. The first event was the more curious. In the morning, the two men who had switched from tailing Maureen Connell to following Sarah Teale arrived at the offices of HCTV and requested an immediate appointment with Nicky Cash. The receptionist, who answered to the name of Tina, was appalled, not so much by the request itself but by the fact that it was only 9 a.m. 'Nicky,' she said artlessly, 'won't be in for ages.'

'When is ages?' replied the taller of the two men.

Tina looked at her watch. She was feeling extremely grumpy this morning, not just because she had a hangover, but because she was used to spending the first hour of her office day drinking coffee, phoning her friends and generally preparing, in a leisurely sort of way, for the rest of the day. It was unheard of to have visitors at this hour. 'Dunno,' she said. 'Ten? Maybe ten-thirty. Depends.'

'It depends on what?' said the smaller man.

Tina looked at him in annoyance. 'On what time he gets up, I s'pose.'

The two men looked at each other. 'Then we'll wait,' said the first one.

'Suit yourselves,' snarled Tina, who was thinking she would be buggered if she was going to make them coffee. Then, as an afterthought, she added, 'Who are you, anyway?' It had just dawned on her that they might be important and therefore not the sort of people in front of whom she should make personal phone calls. Especially the one she had been planning to make to Michelle, who had just acquired a new boyfriend and was never shy of sharing intimate details.

Neither of the men replied, but one of them fished into his breast pocket and produced some ID. Tina gasped when she saw it. This, she thought when she had collected her wits, was just like something out of the movies. She couldn't wait to tell Michelle. Instead, she smiled for the first time that morning and sweetly asked the two men if they would care for some coffee while they were waiting.

The second event concerned Violetta Tapia. At the same time as Tina received her unexpected visitors, Violetta was being collected from hospital by Caterina Portales and driven to the Exile Centre.

Sarah hadn't wasted any time in preparing for her interview. The sooner she got it, the sooner she would be able to get a definite yes out of Nicky Cash and the sooner she could begin her research into the laundering of arms to Iraq, the true story of Chile's involvement in the Falklands War and all the other elements that would contribute to her ground-breaking, sensational documentary. As she headed to the Exile Centre to interview Violetta, she smiled to herself. She was thinking about a conversation she had had last night which would, she was sure, reap great rewards.

Since the death of Danny McLaughlin and the cancellation of the shoot-to-kill documentary, Sarah had rather fallen out with her Government contact, Jeremy Taylor, Although her interview with him had never been shown, he had been nettled by her questions – and especially by her threat to bring forward a witness who would demolish Jeremy's claim that a governmental shoot-to-kill policy was a myth. Sarah, Jeremy had subsequently told her, was getting above herself and he no longer wished to be party to her deviousness. Fine, Sarah had thought – Jeremy was beginning to nauseate her anyway. But much more interestingly, Jeremy was an arch-rival of her Opposition contact, Bob Wilkinson. Bob had often told her how much he would like to find something on Jeremy that would arrest his progress through the ranks of Government. Sarah had that something.

Jeremy had recently made what was, as far as Sarah was concerned, an extremely ill-advised speech in praise of fidelity and family values. Obviously the blonde secretary with whom he was committing adultery had slipped his mind at the time. But she hadn't slipped Sarah's mind. On the phone to Bob the previous night, she had assured him that, in return for a little bit of classified information about the arms to Iraq affair, she would provide him with the wherewithal to end Jeremy's career. She hadn't been particularly proud of herself for doing this, but then, she reasoned, people like Jeremy Taylor ought to know better.

But Sarah herself ought to have known better. By now, her home as well as her office telephone was bugged, and her conversation with Bob Wilkinson had proved of enormous interest to the people who had tapped it. So interesting had they found it that they passed it on to two of their colleagues – the two who were currently sipping Tina's execrable coffee in Nicky Cash's office. Their next port of call after Nicky would be Bob Wilkinson's boss.

Sarah, unaware of this, was feeling enormously pleased with herself about the way things were going. She was even more pleased when, shortly after her arrival at the Chilean Exile Centre, she had Violetta Tapia seated in front of the camera. Violetta proved to be a nervous interviewee but, as far as Sarah was concerned, the more nervous the better. And the fact that Violetta's face was heavily bruised and her lip was cut added greatly to the whole scene. Callous was not a word Sarah would have used to describe herself – unless she was dealing with politicians – but she was, from a professional point of view, rather glad that Violetta had been beaten up. It certainly made her look the part. The producer was, however, full of solicitude as she tried to put the Chilean woman at ease. Her English was good enough for her to be interviewed in that language, but Sarah and Caterina had both decided it would be best if

200

Caterina were to sit in to act as occasional interpreter and constant companion.

For the first few minutes they chatted amiably as Sarah and her team arranged the shoot. The camera would focus exclusively on Violetta and on the object in her lap: the photograph she had waved at Herrera the previous evening. Sarah's first questions as the camera started rolling were about the scene in the banqueting hall and Violetta's treatment at the hands of Herrera's bodyguards. It made a pretty harrowing story and Sarah's sound recordist, no stranger to listening to horror stories, was transfixed. Violetta's lip trembled as she talked about how she had approached Herrera with the photograph of her daughter.

'Tell us,' said Sarah gently, 'about your daughter.'

'My daughter. . . Marcella was working in the human rights office in Santiago. One day she didn't come home from work and I became very worried. Later I receive a phone call from a man who says he saw some men take my daughter from the street in a car. She was screaming that the men were . . . Violetta faltered and turned to Caterina, '*Secuestradome?*'

'Kidnapping.'

'Yes, kidnapping. That the men were kidnapping her.'

'And that was how long ago?'

'Six years.'

'And you haven't seen her since?'

'No. After a month, a man call me and says he has seen Marcella. She was in a secret police house.'

Tears started to well as Violetta continued. 'He said they torture her many times. They put her head in a bucket of – excrement, and then beat her ears until her sense of balance was gone.'

It was not long before Violetta broke down completely and buried her head in her hands. Sarah didn't have the heart to press the woman further. The short, shockingly powerful interview was, anyway, perfect as it was. If it wouldn't convince Nicky Cash that Sarah was on to a winner, then nothing would.

The experience of reliving both the events of the previous night and the horrors of her daughter's disappearance took its toll on Violetta. Exhausted and upset, she was more than happy for Caterina to take her home again immediately after the interview. She declined Caterina's offer to accompany her into the flat. She would, she said, just like to have a rest, if that was going to be at all possible – Violetta's neighbours in the Hackney council block were not known for their silence during the day.

But it wasn't the neighbours who disturbed her. Two minutes after she had entered her bedroom, the doorbell rang. Frowning in irritation, Violetta got off her bed and put her shoes back on. She was not in the mood for visitors. Cautiously opening the front door, she peered into the dark hallway. The man who met her gaze grinned cheerily.

'Morning, madam. Sorry to trouble you. I'm from the council,' he said as he flashed an official-looking identity card at her, 'about the leak in the flat above.'

'Leak?'

'Yes, a water leak. I'm checking that the flats below are all right. Danger of damp, you see. All right if I come in and check here?'

'There's no problem in this flat.'

The man shrugged. 'I'm sure you're right, but it would be best if I check.' Again the impish grin. 'Your carpets could get ruined and you wouldn't want that, would you? It'll only take two minutes.'

Violetta, her initial suspicions crumbling before the man's easy charm, shrugged and let him in. The council had always been extremely helpful to her in the past, and she didn't want to antagonise them by being churlish.

The man walked in, took a damp-meter out of the holdall he was carrying, and set to work. Violetta watched him for a moment as he checked the wall below the window in the sitting-room. Then she went into the kitchen to wash up her breakfast dishes. Watching over him as he went about his business would, she reasoned, look rather rude.

A minute later, the man appeared at the kitchen door. Violetta didn't hear his stealthy tread as she hummed to herself. Nor could she see the expression on his face. The disarming smile had gone, and in its place was a strange and unpleasant look, an expression of smug satisfaction mixed with something approaching pity. Then, after a moment, he coughed and, startled, Violetta turned round. Again he was smiling. 'You were right,' he said, 'nothing to worry about at all.'

'Good. I didn't think there was anything.'

Still smiling, he touched his forehead in a form of salute. 'I'll be off, then.'

As Violetta shut and locked the door behind

him, she felt a sense of unease. She realised she hadn't really checked his identity – and why had he only checked the sitting-room? A life clouded with tragedy and misfortune had made Violetta highly suspicious, and now she suspected the man's story. Worried, and with a frown again creasing her brow, she went into the sitting-room and stared at the place where the man had been checking for damp. Then, suddenly purposeful, she walked over to the sofa against the wall.

Two minutes later, Violetta Tapia's suspicions were confirmed.

19

At the safe house in Berkshire, the morning that was proving so eventful in London became something of a humiliating experience for Tony: he went shopping with Doña Hilda. The General was to spend the day at an Army range on Salisbury Plain, and, just before nine o'clock, Tony and Harry were sitting at the table in the hall finalising the travel arrangements when Doña Hilda swanned past them towards the front door. Tony, puzzled, beckoned to Soledad. 'Where does she think she's going?'

'Er. . . she wants to go shopping.'

'*Shopping*?'

'Yes. In London.'

Tony shook his head. 'Impossible – we don't have any spare manpower.'

Soledad looked at him and arched her eyebrows. 'Just you try telling her that.'

At that moment Herrera came out of the sitting-room. Tony, who had spent half the night regretting his outburst of the previous evening, stood up and addressed him, he hoped, deferentially. 'I'm sorry,' he said, 'but I wasn't told anything about your wife going shopping.'

Herrera shrugged. 'She's only just decided.'

'Well, she'll need protection, and we don't have any to give her.'

Herrera looked coolly at him. 'Perhaps you could accompany her, Mr Clark. You look like the sort of man who knows his way around shops.'

Tony didn't know how to take that one. Soledad, sensing the beginnings of an unpleasant atmosphere, took Tony to one side. 'It's actually not a bad idea.' Tony's expression, however, suggested he thought otherwise. 'I'll come with you,' finished Soledad.

'And who's going to be with Herrera? He has to have one of us as well as his own henchmen.'

Soledad looked at Harry, who was watching the proceedings with amusement. 'I think the General would prefer it if Mr Naylor travelled with him. I really think it would be best.'

Tony was horrified. 'There's no way I'm taking her shopping!'

'Oh, come on, Tony,' interjected Harry, 'hands over the ocean, mate.' Harry too was appalled by the idea of a day spent trailing round Knightsbridge behind the excitable and exhausting Doña Hilda.

Tony glared at him. He was, he knew, beaten. The General had made it perfectly clear that he had no wish for Tony's company but there was no need, he thought, for Harry to gloat. He dropped his hands to his sides in weary resignation. 'All right, all right, I'll go. But don't expect me,' he hissed at Soledad, 'to carry her bloody shopping.'

As both Range Rovers were required for the

General's trip to Wiltshire, Tony ordered a taxi to take his party into town. He sat in moody silence throughout the half-hour trip as Soledad and Doña Hilda chatted at quick-fire speed in Spanish. Watching them covertly, Tony decided that Doña Hilda was an extraordinarily insensitive woman. It was perfectly evident to him that Soledad, despite her politeness, couldn't bear the woman sitting next to her, yet Doña Hilda appeared to be treating her like an old friend. Or maybe, he thought, she was treating her like an old servant.

After they had left the M4 and were approaching Knightsbridge, Doña Hilda became even more animated. The shops that were now coming into view on either side of them were the cause of her excitement and, after a few minutes spent with her nose pressed against the window, she turned to Soledad. '*Preguntale al guardia si sabe donde La Lucia compro su cartera?*'

Soledad couldn't hide her amusement as she looked at Tony. 'She wants to know,' she translated, 'if you've any idea where Mrs Pinochet bought her handbag?'

Tony's thunderous expression was answer enough.

They ended up, like most tourists, in Harrods. Tony hated the place with a vengeance, but had suggested it out of a sense of self-preservation. The huge department store boasted that it could supply you – either immediately or by post – with anything and everything you wanted. He wondered how they would react to a request for a garotte to silence the voluble Chilean whose shopping, an hour later, was now being carried by Tony.

Embarrassed and depressed, Tony trudged after the two women as, with shrieks of delight, Doña Hilda located the Handbag Department. Looking around, Tony reflected that Harrods had been a mistake. It seemed to be stocked with enough handbags to arm every able-bodied woman in South America.

Doña Hilda, however, needed reassurance about her purchase. Tony thought that, by nodding in agreement to everything she pointed out, this mortifying experience would quickly be over. But Doña Hilda soon saw through that one and, evidently dismissing Soledad's taste as too demure, sought the opinions of the saleswomen. They, sensing they had a reckless spendthrift with a bottomless purse on their hands, were only too willing to encourage her.

The handbags – madam hadn't needed much persuasion to purchase several – having been acquired, it became apparent that Doña Hilda was still only warming to her theme. In Harrods she had found her spiritual home, and soon she was leading the hapless Tony through the men's department in search of new outfits for the General. After a few minutes she pounced on a sports jacket and subjected Tony to the ultimate indignity.

Realising that he was almost exactly the same height as her husband, she beckoned him over and held the jacket up against his chest. She was completely oblivious to Tony's total humiliation as she examined the effect. Soledad, who usually betrayed not a flicker of emotion, started giggling. By the time the little party reached the Perfume Hall, Tony was so angry he could barely trust himself to speak. It had been nearly three hours since he'd seen daylight and in that time he'd been bored out of his skull, reduced to a bag-carrier and used as a clothes-horse. The latter had particularly irritated him – it rested uneasily on his conscience to be used as a stand-in for General Herrera. And now he was going to have to put up with the nauseating smell of different scents vying for attention.

But as far as Doña Hilda was concerned, the Perfume Hall was a veritable Aladdin's cave; there was nothing to rival this in the malls of Las Condes in Santiago. She swooped down on one of the counters and began to test various perfumes.

Tony turned grumpily to the equally long-suffering but more stoic Soledad. 'Can't we call it a day?'

Soledad shook her head. 'No. If we do, she'll only want to come back tomorrow. Be patient.'

Tony sighed and shot a murderous look at Doña Hilda. Then, to his horror, he saw a heavily made up girl from one of the sales promotions counters bearing down on them. 'Would you like a make-over, madam?'

Tony moved swiftly to intercept this latest threat. 'No, I'm afraid she doesn't have time.'

The salesgirl, like her colleagues in the Handbag Department, had spotted Doña Hilda from a mile away and wasn't going to be put off by her unpleasant minder. 'I think,' she said haughtily, 'that's for madam to decide, don't you?' Then, replacing her glare with a smile of dazzling intensity, she turned to Doña Hilda. 'Would you like a make-over madam?'

Doña Hilda looked puzzled for a moment. Then, realising what she was being offered, she too became all smiles. 'Un make-over? *Si, si*.'

Tony was now almost hopping with anger and frustration. Soledad tapped him on the arm and whispered, 'Will you please just calm *down*?'

'What she really deserves,' snarled Tony, 'is a make-over like that poor old cow got last night.'

Soledad looked for a moment as if she were about to agree with him, but quickly altered her expression and remained resolutely silent.

Tony, however, now directed his anger at her. During their first few encounters, he had taken her for a strong-minded woman who wouldn't stand for the sort of treatment Doña Hilda was subjecting her to. Now he regarded her as just another subservient acolyte. 'You really do amaze me,' he said with an unpleasant leer.

'Please be quiet.'

'Why the bloody hell should I be bloody quiet? This is *ludicrous*, fawning over some greedy old bitch and her ill-gotten gains.'

Although Soledad had managed to edge Tony away from Doña Hilda and the salesgirl, the latter heard his outburst and looked round in sheer horror. She had established that the woman couldn't speak English and therefore couldn't understand what this ill-bred yob was saying, but *really*.

Soledad was also beginning to find Tony's behaviour unacceptable. 'You should be quiet,' she snapped, 'because you don't understand the situation.'

Tony didn't reply, but his sneering expression seemed to say, 'Oh yeah?'

'Five years ago,' continued Soledad, 'they murdered my brother because he was spraying slogans on a wall.'

'*What*?' Tony was dumbfounded – and completely wrong-footed. He stared at Soledad in amazement. 'You mean—'

'Yes. The secret police shot my brother.'

'So what the hell are you doing trying to keep Herrera alive?' Either Soledad had been brainwashed or there was something he didn't understand.

'Because,' she answered, 'every day the Christian Democrats are in power, the political strength of the military is reduced. And believe me, they know what power is.' She looked thoughtfully over to Doña Hilda. 'If something happened to Herrera, it might just give the military the excuse it needs to mount another coup. And who knows how many people they'll kill then?'

'But surely,' countered Tony, 'the protesters know that too?' Soledad looked witheringly at him. Her words positively dripped with sarcasm as she replied, 'The left don't have a patent on intelligence, Mr Clark.'

Tony looked suitably chastened. Then, as Doña Hilda beckoned to Soledad, he stood alone in the middle of the Harrods Perfume Department and doubted that the day could possibly get any worse.

He was wrong.

Harry was having what he supposed could be

211

described as an 'interesting' day. It was certainly, he didn't doubt, a great deal more interesting than going shopping with Doña Hilda, but he wasn't sure if it was any better for the soul. There was quite a gathering at the military compound on Salisbury Plain. Directors and salesmen from several arms manufacturers as well as some representatives from the British Army were grouped round a marquee watching a weapons demonstration. Herrera, beside Harry, was looking through a pair of binoculars at the activity over the valley below them. His interest in the jet fighter overhead was intense: so was Harry's, but for a different reason. The former was marvelling at the efficacy of the weaponry and its potential benefit to Chile. Harry was wondering for what purpose the weapons would be deployed: another military coup to subjugate Chile's citizens, perhaps?

Both men's thoughts were interrupted by a deep boom as the jet, flashing over its target a mile away, dropped a cluster bomb. Herrera, after a few congratulatory remarks to the men standing on his left, turned to Harry and beamed. Harry didn't beam back.

After a few more demonstrations and an examination, by Herrera, of a glossy brochure on arms produced by the company which had hosted last night's banquet, the group filed into a marquee behind them, where a lavish lunch was being prepared. Harry's expression, often naturally morose, became positively disapproving as he surveyed the feast. No expense, evidently, was being spared.

Miles Courtenay, glad that there had been no unseemly interruptions as at last night's do, was positively glowing as he gave Herrera a sales pitch on his company's latest system. 'We've improved the effectiveness of the weapon,' he said as another distant target was annihilated, 'by approximately ten per cent by reducing the size of the metal fragments.'

Herrera looked with interest at the diagram he was being shown in illustration of the point.

'On level ground,' continued Miles, 'the weapon will now cause serious injury to anyone within a radius of approximately one hundred metres.'

The General nodded his approval. 'Most impressive.'

In his deadpan voice, Miles continued extolling the merits of the weapon. 'The actual lethality figure is relatively low – but of course, that's a benefit.' He smiled in a comradely way at Herrera. 'After all, it requires up to three people to remove and care for each seriously wounded combatant, which stretches the enemy's supply line and diverts resources. All in all, it's a super bit of kit – we're terribly proud of it.'

I bet you are, thought Harry, who was beginning to feel slightly sick. It had never occurred to him before that there were people who were not criminals who spent their entire working lives devising neat little ways to kill other people. Deciding he'd heard enough of Miles Courtenay's self-congratulatory speeches, he moved away. The champagne and smoked salmon at the nearby buffet caught his eye. Perhaps a little sustenance would make him feel less sick. Still, he thought, things could be worse.

He was right.

20

After his exhaustive and exhausing trip round
Harrods, Tony accompanied the ecstatic Doña
Hilda back to the safe house and then, as he was off
duty for a while, went to see Mo. He had been
unable to contact her all day and was anxious to
know if she had unearthed information about any
further surprises the Chilean exiles might be going
to spring on Herrera. In the light of what Soledad
had told him, he fervently hoped there weren't
going to be any.

Mo, however, had a surprise of a different sort
in store for him.

'You're doing *what*?' he said when she told him.

'I'm quitting.'

'But why? You can't just walk out like that.'
Tony, initially, wasn't so much annoyed as puzzled.
It was unheard of for Mo to quit in the middle of a
job.

Mo looked defiantly at him. 'I'm afraid I can
Tony, and I'm going to.'

'I don't understand.'

'This morning,' she explained, 'I was at the Exile
Centre and I saw that Violetta Tapia woman there.

214

She looked as if she was at death's door, Tony.'

'I —'

'And I also heard what she was saying to Sarah.'

'To Sarah?'

'Yes. She was interviewing her for her film. It was ghastly, Tony. I couldn't believe that supposedly sane people could actually do things like that. I mean, the things she was saying . . .' Mo trailed off, unable to stomach any repetition of the atrocities Violetta had related.

Tony waved his arms in the air helplessly. 'Look, I'm not responsible —'

'But you *are*, Tony. You're responsible for Herrera's security, and Herrera's ultimate responsible for what those people did to that woman — not to mention her daughter.' She glared at him in fury. 'How on earth can you carry on working for him?'

Tony glared back. 'You've got a responsibility to finish the job, Mo.'

'Bullshit! I didn't sign up for this to let old women be battered half to death.'

'And neither did I!' Then Tony took a deep breath and added, more calmly, 'But we're not responsible for what's happened — *they* are. And anyway, those things could get worse if we quit. It's just a job, Mo.'

'Well, it's not the kind of job I want.'

But, she asked herself as Tony walked out in disgust, what kind of job *did* she want? Kate had badgered her to apply for all manner of things that looked suitable — and boring — and had then gone bananas when, on returning from her business trip, she had found Mo working for Tony yet again. That had led to another argument and further deterioration of the atmosphere in the house they had bought together with such high hopes. 'It's just this once,' Mo had said to her girlfriend.

'Oh yes? Just like the other time?' was Kate's tart reply.

Yet Mo hadn't banked on the Herrera job opening her eyes quite so much to the violence and gross iniquities of the Chilean military regime. She should, she realised, have obeyed her first instincts when Tony had offered her the job. Seeing Violetta Tapia's injuries and listening to her heart-rending words had been the last straw. She couldn't, she knew, continue working on this job and still emerge with her conscience intact.

As she watched Tony stomp down the street towards his car, Mo wondered if she'd finally burned her boats with him. Suddenly she felt cold. The thought of never working with Tony or Harry again was a deeply upsetting one. Would she now have to condemn herself to spending the next thirty years of her life stuck in some awful office arguing about the coffee rota?

Tony, uncharacteristically, started worrying about his health. He had spent most of the day in a rage and now, after the episode with Mo, he could almost feel his blood boiling. Letting himself into his flat, he reflected that the cigarette he was smoking – and he had been chain-smoking since leaving Harrods – was not helping the situation. And the drink, the several drinks, he so desperately craved would no doubt send him back to Charing Cross Hospital: not as a visitor but as a heart-attack victim.

Slamming the front door behind him, he realised that he would be spared his heart-attack: he would have to drive back to the safe house for night duty, and turning up drunk would put the final nail in the coffin of his relationship with Herrera. Instead, he sighed and went into the kitchen to make himself a cup of tea. Then he wondered what to do next. There was a multitude of things he could have been doing, foremost of which was to tidy the flat. Looking around, he reflected that the large, airy and sparsely furnished bachelor pad he had bought only a year ago because of its style was now looking distinctly unstylish. It was the sort of place that required the regular ministrations of a cleaner, someone he didn't have. It was also the sort of flat that didn't lend itself to being a place of business as well as a home and, of course, it now had to cater for both functions. Walking back into the sitting-room, he glanced at the new fax machine and answerphone. Both were dormant, and there were no flashing lights to indicate that prospective clients had been beating down the doors of Tony Clark Associates. Tony felt like hurling both machines out the window.

Thoroughly fed up now, he succumbed – as he was prone to doing in times of stress – to the lure of another machine. Pulling off his jacket, tie and shoes, he slumped full-length on the sofa and picked up the TV remote control. He didn't care what was on. He was in the mood to watch anything, and if it was mindless rubbish then so much the better. The programme he randomly selected *was* mindless rubbish, but Tony was blissfully unaware of that fact. Almost immediately, he fell asleep.

He was woken by the sound of the doorbell. The one thing he had meant to change on buying the flat was the unpleasantly jarring chime of the bell. Even his neighbours had complained about the sound, so it had become something of a reflex action for him to answer it at once. In an even worse temper than ever now that his slumbers had been disturbed, he padded to the front door and, unnecessarily aggressively, threw it open. Sarah Teale was standing on the threshold. He looked at her for a moment. 'What,' he said coldly, 'are *you* doing here?' Sarah had not exactly expected him to ooze charm, but she was more than a little thrown by his greeting. There were, she thought, limits to how rude one should be.

'I need to talk to you,' she said quickly.

'What about?'

'Violetta Tapia.' She looked imploringly at him. 'Please, Tony, I wouldn't be here if it wasn't important.'

Tony considered for a split-second before relenting and letting her in. In the light of their current so-called relationship, he knew her errand must be serious. Sarah, he had to admit, had a healthy respect for her own pride. He ushered her into the sitting-room and, despite himself, smiled as he saw her appraising look. Sarah's first visit to his flat should have been in altogether different circumstances: dinner, wine and candlelight had been what he had originally envisaged, not the argument which he was sure was about to take place. It

218

was, however, reassuring that she obviously liked the place.

Tony motioned to one of the low sofas. 'Well?'

Sarah sat down, rummaged in her handbag and produced a small object wrapped in tissue paper which she handed to Tony. Giving her a quizzical look, but without saying anything, he unwrapped the little parcel to reveal a spent shell case. He twirled it round in his fingers, identifying it as coming from a small hand-gun, and looked again at Sarah.

'Violetta,' she said in answer to his questioning look, 'found it hidden in her flat. Someone planted it under the cushions of her sofa.'

'Who?'

'A man arrived, apparently, saying he was from the council about some damp or something. Violetta let him in —'

'She should have asked him for some identification.'

Sarah looked at him in exasperation. 'Are you going to let me finish or are you just going to interrupt all the time?'

'Sorry, sorry.' Tony raised an appeasing hand.

'He did, so she said, show some identification, but Violetta didn't get a chance to look at it too closely. Remember,' she added tartly, 'she's not that great at reading English. She wouldn't have wanted to embarrass herself. Anyway, the point is, she phoned me after she found this and I checked with the council. They hadn't sent anybody. Hadn't a clue what I was talking about.'

Tony mused over the implications of that one for a moment. Then, frowning, he turned to

Sarah. 'If I'm reading this correctly, then the gun that fired this,' he indicated the shell, 'is going to be used to shoot Herrera. But why on earth would one of the exiles want to set up Violetta Tapia? She's *one* of them, for Christ's sake. It just doesn't make sense.'

'It does if the man who planted it isn't one of the exiles.'

Tony, remembering his recent conversation with Soledad and her indication that the military were itching to mount another coup, looked sharply at Sarah. 'You mean it could be the far right stirring up trouble? But why on earth would they want to do in their own man?'

Sarah smiled grimly. 'Believe it or not, Tony, in Santiago Herrera is considered something of a moderate. There are groups out there who believe Hitler's deepest flaw was his compassion for humanity.'

Again Tony looked at her, but he didn't reply. There wasn't much to say.

'So,' continued Sarah, 'they kill Herrera, blame the left, and all hell breaks loose in Santiago. Bingo! Another military coup.'

Tony now looked doubtful. 'I've got to say, I find that pretty incredible.'

Sarah sighed. 'When I was in Santiago before the elections that Pinochet thought he was going to win, the military junta's news agency put out a story about a bomb exploding outside the Government building – half an hour before it went off.' She looked pointedly at Tony. 'They do, you see, know what they're doing.'

Tony, having thought that Herrera was

responsible for all the evils that had ever happened in Chile, was now forced to contemplate the unappetising possibility that even he, Pinochet's deputy, could be used as a pawn in a dangerous, deadly game.

Sarah, misinterpreting his silence, sought to extend an olive branch to him. 'Tony, I know that what happened wasn't your fault. You were only doing your job.' She paused and then continued. 'I just hope you understand that I'm just trying to do mine.'

And who was to say, thought Tony, which job was the more important? He grinned. 'Yeah, I do.'

The atmosphere between them, no longer one of overt antagonism, was still uneasy. 'I've got to go soon, I'm on night duty.'

Sarah too got up. She walked to the door and flashed him what she hoped was a placatory smile. 'I'll see you, then.'

'Yeah. Bye.'

21

The atmosphere between Harry and the Chilean guards had, after their day at Salisbury Plain, thawed somewhat. All the men had been bored and, for want of anything better to do, had started talking again. The fact that Harry's conversations with all of them bar del Canto consisted mainly of sign language probably helped rather than hindered the situation. He wouldn't, he thought, relish getting into any serious political conversations with them. But, as they sat in the small sitting-room of the safe house that evening, Harry reckoned there would anyway be no danger of that happening. These men hadn't been hired for their intellectual abilities.

They did, however, have abilities in other directions. Harry was rather surprised to see how much whisky they were putting away that evening – and even more surprised to see Osvaldo del Canto entering the room with two more bottles. He waved them in their faces and said, in Spanish, that they were a present from the General who, he added with a pointed look at Harry 'never forgot his men'. The implication was clear: Osvaldo evidently thought that Tony didn't do a very good job of remembering Harry. Then the Chileans settled down to watch the football on television. It didn't seem to matter that they were watching Manchester United versus Chelsea.

Football, any football, was practically a religion in South America. And since Brazil had won the 1994 World Cup, that religion had become even more popular. Antonio, with the smile that always managed to look like a snarl, offered a tumbler of whisky to Harry, who regretfully shook his head. He was on duty for another hour until Tony took over, and then he had to drive back to London. With a friendly nod at the Chileans, he got up and went back to the security room. Almost as soon as he entered the room, his pager bleeped, indicating that someone had left a message with his answering service. He reached for the telephone beside the security control panel and dialled the service, then frowned in irritation as he listened to the message. Bugger it, he thought, what do I do now?

Practically before he had replaced the receiver, del Canto entered the room. 'I thought you might like to know the score,' he said with a friendly grin.

'Oh. Yeah.'

Harry, thought del Canto looked distracted. 'Everything all right?' he asked.

'Yeah – well, no.'

'What is it?'

'My neighbour,' said Harry, 'has just called to say my burglar alarm's gone off.' He shrugged. 'It's never gone off by accident before.'

'Oh, I see.' Del Canto, looking thoughtful,

appeared to share Harry's concern. 'Look,' he said suddenly, 'Why don't you go and sort it out? I can watch the house while you're away.'

Harry looked gratefully at the big Chilean. Ever since Joyce had died, Harry's house had begun to feel like a grave. He couldn't bear the thought of that grave being desecrated by burglars. 'Would you really?' He stood up. 'That'd be good of you.' He shrugged in a slightly embarrassed fashion. 'If it's burglars, I'd like to get the bastards with my own hands, if you know what I mean.'

Del Canto clapped him on the back. 'No problem, Harry.'

Harry walked to the door. 'I'll only be gone about an hour, and Tony should be here not long after that.' Then, suddenly remembering something, he fished in his pocket and produced a key. 'You'd better take this.'

Del Canto, only mildly interest, took the proffered key to the alarm system. 'Oh yes. Thanks.' Then, with a nonchalant wave to Harry, he settled down in front of the security cameras and produced a comic from his pocket.

As soon as Harry had shut the door behind him, del Canto put the comic away again and watched the screens intently. Soon Harry came into view, got into his car and headed down the drive. Del Canto waited for a few minutes, picked up the key and went over to the control panel. In one deft movement, he switched off the entire alarm system protecting the safe house. Then he left the security room and went into the hall. For a few moments he stared at the door of the room where the other guards were drinking and watching the football and, with a thoughtful expression on his face, he crossed to the door of the lounge and opened it quietly. Herrera, with a glass of whisky at his side, was contentedly playing chess by himself in the far corner of the room. Del Canto, unseen by the General, quickly closed the door again and made straight for the staircase. Swiftly and silently, he padded upstairs and walked softly along the landing to the General's bedroom. The door was open and inside, an excited Doña Hilda was sorting through her purchases. Judging from her expression, del Canto reckoned she would be playing with them for some time. Not that, if things went like clockwork, they would need a lot of time.

Harry, intent on reaching London as quickly as possible, failed to notice the car parked almost under the overhanging trees in the layby near the house. Ten seconds after he shot past it, the door opened and out stepped the blond man who had that morning visited Violetta Tapia. And he was carrying a Czech-made hand-gun which used the same kind of bullet as he had planted in Violetta's sofa.

The man ran swiftly along the road and turned into the drive from which Harry had exited only moments before. Dressed entirely in black, he melted into the night as he jogged towards the house. Inside the security room, the video screens picked up his image, yet the alarms remained mute. Looking at his watch as he reached the house, the man ran round to the garage door. It was serious-looking, and reinforced with steel. It

225

was also unlocked. Two seconds later the intruder, undetected, was inside the safe house.

Sarah's visit had seriously alarmed Tony. Coupled with Mo's refusal to carry on working on this job, it augured very ill indeed. The planting of the bullet at Violetta's house meant that someone, somehow, was planning to kill Herrera and blame it on the exiles. Tony didn't doubt that, after Herrera's death, more evidence would be found that would incriminate Violetta and some of her compatriots from the Exile Centre. But who was masterminding the operation? If Mo hadn't run out on him, he would have put her on to the case: he would have asked her to get anything and everything available on Herrera's entourage and any other right-wing Chileans currently in London. Yet even as he thought about it, he knew that such a brief would have yielded too little, too late. Herrera was leaving tomorrow, so if anything was going to happen, it was going to happen tonight.

His face creased with anxiety, he stamped on the accelerator and drove along the M4 as quickly as he dared. It really would be the last straw, he thought, if he got caught for speeding. In his early days in the force, he had heard all manner of excuses for doing over a ton, but his own would really take the biscuit. 'You're trying to stop a Chilean general from being assassinated? Is that right, Mr Clark? In *Berkshire*?' He could just imagine the hoots of derision with which the motorway police would greet that one. He was also now beginning to curse his own stubbornness in insisting on a safe house rather than an hotel. If Herrera had been, as his

226

wife had so fervently wished, based in Claridges, then Tony would have had no trouble phoning Harry to tell him to be on his guard. As it was, there was no way he could phone him at the safe house: there were any number of extensions, and any number of prying ears to listen in on them.

So intent was he on reaching the safe house as fast as possible that, shortly after he turned off the motorway, he failed to notice Harry's car speeding past him in the other direction.

When he reached his destination, he realised that he'd better calm down. There was no point in roaring up the drive and bursting through the front door like a lunatic. He must make his arrival look as normal as possible. The fact that he was nearly an hour early would surprise nobody: del Canto, he knew, already had him written down as completely paranoid. So, parking his car neatly round the side as he usually did, he sauntered up to the front door. It was, as it should have been, securely locked. He rang the bell for Harry to let him in. After two rings he became slightly impatient; after four his face, picked up on one of the screens in the empty security room, betrayed serious anxiety. Quickly coming to a decision, he ran round to the back door. It was, to his horror, unlocked. Rushing into the house, Tony went straight into the security room.

'What the fuck . . .?' he yelled to himself as he took in the scene. Not only was the room empty, but the security system had been disarmed and the key removed. He looked around in puzzlement, almost as if he expected Harry to be hiding in the tiny room. And then he saw something moving on one of the video screens. Tony peered closely and moaned softly in mingled horror and disbelief. The picture showed a blond man dressed in black and carrying a gun – and he was heading towards the lounge. Tony slammed his fist against the emergency alarm button. Nothing happened. Then he steeled himself and walked out of the room. He had, he supposed, the element of surprise, but what he really needed was a gun.

Edging round the side of the hall, he was just in time to see the man coming out of the lounge. Everything about his stance told Tony that he still hadn't located his target, and it was quite evident that the gun still hadn't been fired. Tony breathed a sigh of relief. Herrera was normally drinking an apéritif in the lounge at this time in the evening. Then, just as Tony was beginning to realise that he didn't stand a chance against this man, the General appeared from the kitchen. The blond man, as yet unseen by his prey, lifted the gun and took aim.

Tony, moving faster than he'd ever done in his life, launched himself out of his hiding-place and flew at the man. Throwing his entire body weight against him, he knocked him completely off his feet only a split-second before the gun went off. The shot, muted by the silencer, hit the wall as Herrera, open-mouthed and rigid with shock, stared at the scene before him.

The intruder was clearly supremely fit and extremely well trained. He recovered from the surprise of Tony's attack and, with extraordinary agility, managed to leap back to his feet while raining vicious blows at Tony's head. Instinctively trying to protect himself, Tony lost his hold on the man and he fled down the hall, pulled open a curtain and tried to smash the small window beside the front door. The toughened glass, however, resisted his frenzied blows.

Tony knew the man wasn't going to get away: Tony now had the gun. He walked down the hall as the man, suddenly aware of his plight, looked feverishly around him for a means of escape. There was to be no escape. Like a rabbit transfixed by car headlights, he looked at Tony in terror. Tony smiled grimly. He had no intention of shooting the man: apart from the fact that it would no longer be in self-defence, the man was too valuable. He knew too much. Tony looked forward to the results of his questioning, and to the extra-ordinary element that the attempted shooting would provide in Sarah's film about Chile. Suddenly he very much wanted her programme to be made. Surely it would go a long way to exposing the evil and awful power that the military still held in Chile? Surely it would help people like Violetta Tapia? And if it would help make a hero out of Herrera, then he could accept that. Whoever had organised this little episode obviously thought that Herrera was easily expendable – and far too liberal. The man who had his terrorised gaze fixed on Tony and the gun would be able to name names.

With these thoughts flashing through his mind in an instant, Tony raised the gun and barked at the man to stay where he was. The intruder had no intention of disobeying – he even put up his hands in a gesture of surrender. It did him little good: ten seconds later a small, perfectly round hole appeared in the middle of his forehead, his mouth opened in a mute 'O' of surprise – and then he died. Tony, and Herrera behind him, watched in astonishment as he slumped to the ground like a rag doll. Tony even looked in disbelief at the gun he was holding, thinking for a split second that it had gone off of its own volition. But he knew it hadn't: someone else had shot the intruder. Turning round, he saw Osvaldo del Canto standing on the bottom step of the staircase holding a pistol. There was a brief silence while the reality of the situation set in. It was del Canto who broke it.

'*Está bien, General?*' he asked coolly.

Herrera, still trying to take in what had happened, nodded slowly. '*Sí, sí.*'

Tony caught del Canto's eye. For the first time since they had met, there was a perfect understanding between them. The gleam in del Canto's dark, beady eyes told Tony all he needed to know, and the twisted smile on his cruel lips confirmed it.

22

'Look,' said Tony as they waited at the Heathrow VIP Centre the next day. 'Mr Naylor says he gave the key to del Canto and . . .' he paused for emphasis as he looked Herrera in the eye, 'and I believe him.'

Herrera's answer was nothing if not direct. 'So do I,' he said simply.

Then both men looked towards the plane standing on the tarmac. Del Canto, with his customary swagger was checking Doña Hilda's many suitcases before they were loaded into the hold of Herrera's plane. He was, interestingly, surrounded by members of the Chilean armed forces who had arrived with the plane. Clearly, he was being closely monitored. And even more clearly, the look in Herrera's eye indicated that, once back in Chile, the man's days would be numbered.

Herrera then turned back to Tony and, with a warm smile, extended his hand. 'Thank you for your help, Mr Clark.' Tony looked slightly embarrassed and didn't quite meet his eye. 'Yeah. . . well,' he mumbled.

'Goodbye,' said Herrera, and walked out of the lounge and out of Tony's life.

Tony watched him for a moment with an unfathomable expression on his face and then squared his shoulders and heaved a huge sigh of relief. Harry and Henry Goode, who had been watching the little scenario wih interest, walked up to him.

'Everything all right?' asked Henry brightly. The man, thought Tony with annoyance, always looked unnecessarily cheerful.

'No,' he replied, 'it's not. I still can't believe you're letting del Canto get away with it. He shot a man in cold blood. He should at least be questioned.'

Henry shrugged. 'Even if we wanted to we couldn't. You know he's got diplomatic status. Let's just forget about it, OK?' He smiled again. 'You've done a great job. The guys upstairs are really impressed – so don't go and blow it now.'

Tony looked sick to the stomach. He realised full well that he was being congratulated for keeping quiet, for being a bastard; for a tacit agreement that he wouldn't make trouble and report the incident at the safe house to anyone who might make waves.

It had all been handled smoothly by Henry and 'the boys upstairs'. Immediately after del Canto had shot the intruder, Tony, as per his instructions in an emergency, had phoned Henry Goode. Half an hour after his call, an unmarked ambulance and a team from MI5 had appeared on the scene. A few minutes after their arrival, Harry had returned from London in almost as much of a state of anxiety as Tony had been in earlier. His burglar alarm had gone off not by accident, not because someone was trying to burgle his house, but because someone had smashed the alarm box itself. As pointless crimes went, that one took the biscuit. Only as he started on his journey back to Berkshire did he begin to think that there might, after all, have been a motive behind that peculiar act. It had been a very easy and very effective way of getting him out of the safe house for an hour.

His worst fears were confirmed when he saw the extra vehicles parked outside on his return. Soon he joined Henry, Herrera, del Canto and Tony in the lounge as Henry tried to establish what had happened. It proved to be impossible. Del Canto vehemently denied that Harry had given him the key to the security system, and when the key was subsequently found underneath the table in the security room by one of Henry's men, there seemed little point in debating the matter further. Herrera had remained very quiet throughout the proceedings and, after gazing thoughtfully at del Canto for a while, had said that he would retire to comfort his wife who, on hearing the shot fired by del Canto, had rushed downstairs and contributed greatly to the ensuing mayhem.

The other guards had been less than helpful. As they had all been off duty, they had, they claimed, been justified in getting drunk in the little sitting-room. And no, they hadn't heard anything above the noise of the television. Only del Canto's shot had finally brought them out of the room.

Both Tony and Harry had been nearly struck

dumb by the way Henry had handled the situation. He quickly established that nobody had the faintest idea of the identity of the intruder, that his target had unquestionably been Herrera, and that the security system had been left unarmed and unmanned due to an unfortunate oversight. During his weighing up of the situation, he had repeatedly glanced in Tony and Harry's direction. His expression had been friendly enough, but the look in his eyes spoke volumes. 'Keep quiet,' it said. 'I'll do this my way.'

His way involved leaving the MI5 officers in situ for extra security and taking the body away in the unmarked ambulance. Tony knew with a sinking heart that it would also involve making sure that the incident was not reported in the customary way: no mention of it would ever appear in the press. It would be as if nothing had ever happened.

The most galling thing about that, thought Tony as he walked out of the VIP Centre, was that Henry knew exactly what had happened. It was so patently obvious that del Canto had masterminded the attempted assassination of Herrera, but Henry continued to smile blandly and insist that Tony had done a fine job. Herrera, after all, was still alive, wasn't he? Henry left them outside the VIP Centre. He shook hands with both Tony and Harry. 'I'll be in touch,' was his parting shot.

Tony looked bleakly at his departing back. He had a nasty feeling that it was true. Henry *would* be in touch and Tony Clark Associates would find themselves involved, yet again, in helping the people who upheld Britain's laws either to ignore them or break them. He felt almost physically sick.

'I need a drink,' he said to Harry. 'I need many drinks.'

Harry looked laconically at him. 'There's half a bottle of whisky at the house.'

'Shame to waste it.'

Sarah Teale, ignorant of the events which had taken place at the safe house the previous night, and indeed of Herrera's departure, returned to see Nicky Cash at HCTV that day. She was extremely pleased with her brief interview with Violetta Tapia and reckoned it made an arresting focal point to her proposed documentary. She was, however, less sure about how to act on the information she had later gleaned from Violetta about the shell she had found in her flat. To regale Nicky Cash about a forthcoming assassination attempt on Herrera would probaby be to say the least, a little misguided. If an attempt was made – or indeed, if he were actually killed by the right-wingers – then so much the better for her programme. As it was, she had enough angles to the documentary. It would have been gratifying, however, to be already in possession of some information from Bob Wilkinson. She had tried to arrange a meeting with him earlier in the day, and had been puzzled by the fact that her repeated attempts to phone his private line had led her to the operator, who had informed her that the line was unobtainable. Sarah was irritated but not too perturbed by that: no doubt she would be able to contact him later.

Fifteen minutes after entering the offices of HCTV she was showing the rough cut of the Violetta Tapia interview to Cash and the frightful

Jessica. They sat together in front of the video while Sarah, discreetly watching Nicky out of the corner of her eye, sat slightly apart. Violetta, she had to admit, came over convincingly powerfully – and as a most distressing sight.

'He said they torture her many times. They put her head in a bucket of – excrement and then beat her ears until her sense of balance was gone . . .' On screen, Violetta's bruises from her own beating at the hands of Herrera's guards looked even more livid than they had in the flesh. Sarah felt like crying when the woman finished with the heart-felt: 'I never saw my daughter again.'

Nicky Cash also felt like crying: not just because of Violetta's impassioned words, but because he was going to have to turn down what he was sure would be the most brilliant and controversial documentary he had ever seen.

When he had sauntered into the office the previous day at the congenial hour of eleven o'clock, he had been more than a little taken aback to find that two men from MI5 were waiting to see him. At first, he had been rather alarmed by the news; then it had begun to appeal to his vanity.

Obviously, they were coming to see him because they were going to ask him to do something secret and hugely important. Ten minutes into their conversation, it became apparent that this was not the case. Nicky, for all his assumed bravado, was something of a coward and actually became rather frightened. Sarah Teale, the men warned him, was skating on dangerously thin ice and was beginning to pose a threat to national security. Her sources, they said, were unreliable and many of her ideas unsubstantiated. In short, and in the interests of the Government, the film must never be made.

Nicky, being Nicky, replied that he had no intention of accepting it anyway. Ingratiatingly, he told them that he had already decided Sarah's proposals were both naive and subversive. The men from MI5, deeply unimpressed by Nicky, took their leave, suggesting as they did so that Nicky shouldn't, of course, tell Sarah the real reasons for his rejection of her programme. Nicky, by now terrified, said that of course he wouldn't. The three of them hadn't even met, had they? The men from MI5 rather relished the thought of never having met Nicky.

Slowly, he turned round to face Sarah a few seconds after Violetta's image had faded from the screen. Neither he nor Jessica said a word and Sarah, unnerved by their silence, couldn't stop herself from babbling. 'Obviously, it's only a rough cut, and it can be tightened up a lot, but I think the structure works.'

There was still no response from either of them. Sarah, annoyance now beginning to overtake her unease, looked at Jessica. Jessica looked at Nicky. Earlier that morning, he had instructed her to leave all the talking to him. When she had repeatedly challenged him as to why, he had eventually told her about the men from MI5. He reckoned it would have come out anyway: Jessica was always telling him he talked in his sleep. That, of course, had led him to the question of whether or not to tell his wife.

Finally he spoke. His expression was as disdainful as the tone of his words. 'Where are the bodyguards? I thought this was a film about bodyguards?'

'Exactly,' said Jessica. 'This isn't what we agreed.'

Nicky glared at her and then carried on. 'No, it bloody well isn't,' he said. 'And who *is* that old woman anyway?'

Sarah was momentarily stunned into silence. Hadn't they been listening to a word she had said? 'Violetta Tapia's story was so moving,' she said evenly, 'that the film naturally came together round her. When we add the true, awful statistics about Chile's human rights record and our Government's duplicity in dealing with them and then the Herrera story, Violetta's story will be even more moving. And —'

But Nicky had had enough. He stood up, took Sarah's video out of the recorder, and handed it to her. 'You may find it moving, but as far as I'm concerned it's yesterday's news. And it's also bloody depressing.'

'Exactly,' said Jessica.

Sarah was so thrown by the reaction she got from Nicky Cash that she took herself off to a wine bar and sank a large glass of extremely expensive Chablis in five minutes flat. She simply couldn't believe what had happened. The programme, she knew, was going to be dynamite. What had he said: depressing and yesterday's news? The man was obviously losing his touch. After another glass of wine and half an hour of serious contemplation, she decided that maybe Cash had been so negative because he didn't believe she could substantiate her story about Chile colluding with Britain in the

Falklands War and about the laundering of arms to Iraq. Perhaps she ought to start researching those aspects of the documentary and then present the idea to buyers to other TV companies. She had, she told herself, always thought Nicky Cash was a jerk anyway, and couldn't understand his apparently meteoric rise to success in the television world. And as for the unspeakable Jessica . . .

Sarah weaved out of the wine bar and decided to make another stab at phoning Bob Wilkinson. Surely the Government, of all institutions, ought to be able to get its telephone systems sorted out fairly promptly. On her way to the phone box on the opposite corner, she stopped to buy an evening paper. She knew from experience that most of what it contained would be of little interest to her, yet she somehow found herself buying a copy every day. It was the thought that maybe, just maybe, there would be something in it for her that kept her going.

Today her wish came true. She opened the paper and almost the first thing that leaped to her attention was the surprise resignation of Bob Wilkinson. Her mouth hanging open in disbelief, Sarah read that he was leaving 'to spend more time with his family'. She was so shocked that a couple of passers-by actually stopped to ask her if everything was all right. Barely registering their concern, all she could do was nod dumbly. She tried to tell herself that there could be a multitude of reasons why he had resigned, yet something deep inside her knew the truth. The coincidence was too great. Someone, she now realised, had got to Nicky Cash to tell him to have nothing more to do with Sarah Teale. And she didn't doubt that that same person had got wind of her conversation with Bob, and forced him to resign. What was it that Mo had said to her when she had first evinced interest in making a programme about Chile? 'Christ, Sarah! You really relish playing with fire, don't you?'

Sarah shivered. Suddenly she realised just what a dangerous game she had been playing. And then she thought about Tony. Had she, through her contact with him, brought trouble his way as well?

Three hours later she knew the answer. She knew all about the assassination attempt, about del Canto masterminding it, and about the departure of the General and his party. She also knew that she had no intention of even telling anyone about the entire affair, far less of making a documentary about it. Furthermore, she knew that she would soon be incapable of walking in a straight line.

She and Tony were sprawled on the large sofa in his sitting-room, a nearly empty bottle of whisky on the table in front of them. He, after his earlier stint with Harry, had been well on the way to getting drunk when he had answered the door to her ring, smiled sweetly, and apologised for the fact that he was dressed only in a T-shirt and boxer shorts. 'I'm plastered,' he had said as if that explained it. And when he told Sarah his side of the story, she too expressed a strong desire to get plastered. Tony, his hand alarmingly unsteady, sloshed more neat whisky into their empty glasses. 'I should point out,' he slurred, 'that my chances of vomiting in the nesht hour are quite high.' Then, as they both knocked back the drinks in one gulp, he flung his arm around her and tried to focus on her face. 'In fact, I hate to disappoint you, but even intercourse is beyond me in my current shtate.'

Sarah pulled herself free from his embrace and grinned wickedly. She reached for the bottle and poured two more drinks. Then she looked him straight in the eye. 'Your call, Tony.'

BETWEEN THE LINES
BREAKING POINT

Diane Pascal

SOME POLICEMEN THINK THEY HAVE
ABSOLUTE POWER. THE POWER TO CORRUPT
ABSOLUTELY ...

And it's the job of the C.I.B. – the Complaints
Investigation Bureau – to tackle that corruption within
the Force. So when trouble looms in Liverpool, Tony
Clark, Harry Naylor and Maureen Connell are sent to
shoot it.

They get more than they bargained for. Unpleasant
details emerge about the city's most respected policeman;
confessions are found to be extracted under force; and a
first class woman journalist goes beyond the call of duty –
and straight into the arms of Tony Clark. And back in
London, the aftermath of a riot invites more doubts about
police brutality, about racism and about a vital piece of
evidence that could implicate someone very high up in
the Met ...

FICTION
0 7515 0695 8

BETWEEN THE LINES
THE CHILL FACTOR
Tom McGregor

NOBODY'S ABOVE THE LAW. AND EVEN IN
THE POLICE FORCE, NOBODY'S ABOVE
SUSPICION ...

A policeman's lot is not a happy one – especially if you're
Detective Superintendent Tony Clark. Tough, dynamic
and highly professional, he's also pretty unpopular. For
like all his colleagues, he's there to tackle criminals. But
unlike them, his targets are criminals who have another,
highly respectable job. They're policemen ...

With his deputy Harry Naylor and Sergeant Maureen
Connell, Clark is used to corruption in high places. But
this time the stakes are higher. Much higher. For
suddenly an ongoing case, a catastrophe in his already
complex personal life, a prostitute, a murder and a
blackmailing porn-merchant become linked by one
thread. And at the end of that thread is one of the most
powerful men in the police force. A man who has covered
his tracks so well that he reckons he's untouchable.
Fireproof. Invincible. But he's reckoned without
Tony Clark ...

FICTION
0 7515 0696 6

Warner now offers an exciting range of quality titles by both established and new authors. All of the books in this series are available from:
Little, Brown and Company (UK),
P.O. Box 11,
Falmouth,
Cornwall TR10 9EN.

Alternatively you may fax your order to the above address. Fax No. 0326 376423.

Payments can be made as follows: Cheque, postal order (payable to Little, Brown and Company) or by credit cards, Visa/Access. Do not send cash or currency. UK customers: and B.F.P.O.: please send a cheque or postal order (no currency) and allow £1.00 for postage and packing for the first book, plus 50p for the second book, plus 30p for each additional book up to a maximum charge of £3.00 (7 books plus).

Overseas customers including Ireland, please allow £2.00 for postage and packing for the first book, plus £1.00 for the second book, plus 50p for each additional book.

NAME (Block Letters) ....

ADDRESS...

....

☐ I enclose my remittance for _____

☐ I wish to pay by Access/Visa Card

Number ☐☐☐☐☐☐☐☐☐☐☐☐☐☐☐☐

Card Expiry Date ☐☐☐☐